WEST

JANELLA CHAPPELL

Author's Tranquility Press
ATLANTA, GEORGIA

Copyright © 2023 by Janella Chappell

All rights reserved. No part of this publication may be reproduced, distributed or transmitted in any form or by any means, including photocopying, recording, or other electronic or mechanical methods, without the prior written permission of the publisher, except in the case of brief quotations embodied in critical reviews and certain other noncommercial uses permitted by copyright law. For permission requests, write to the publisher, addressed "Attention: Permissions Coordinator," at the address below.

Janella Chappell/ Author's Tranquility Press
3800 Camp Creek Pkwy SW Bldg. 1400-116 #1255
Atlanta, GA 30331, USA
www.authorstranquilitypress.com

Publisher's Note: This is a work of fiction. Names, characters, places, and incidents are a product of the author's imagination. Locales and public names are sometimes used for atmospheric purposes. Any resemblance to actual people, living or dead, or to businesses, companies, events, institutions, or locales is completely coincidental.

Ordering Information:
Quantity sales. Special discounts are available on quantity purchases by corporations, associations, and others. For details, contact the "Special Sales Department" at the address above.

WEST/Janella Chappell
Paperback: 978-1-962492-05-8
eBook: 978-1-962492-06-5

On a Summer evening near the cave run lake, Quinn Wincott, Taylor Malone, Maya Post, Ashely Platts, and Emily Atchison were having a good time outside around the campfires. Blake Lawton, Pacey Wheeler, Caden Maguire, Trey Banks, Parker Weber, and A.J. West were talking. They were sitting on a Log. Blake kept looking at Quinn. Caden said, "Blake, Go to Quinn." Blake was looking at Caden, Ehen Quinn. Blake said, "No!' Caden said, "Why not?" Blake said, "Quinn has a boyfriend, Ryan." Caden said, "No, I think they broke up." Blake said, "How do you know?" Caden said, "J. was there. They were arguing. Ryan didn't want Quinn to come here." Blake said, "Why didn't Ryan want Quinn to come here? Ryan should let Quinn come here to have a good time." Caden said, "Ryan knew that Quinn really likes you." Blake said, "Yeah, right." Caden said, "Not lying, Quinn really likes you, Quinn kept looking at you, and you kept looking at Quinn too." said, "Quinn does like you, Blake, Quinn is trying to make you jealous. That's why Quinn is dating Ryan." Blake was quiet. Blake kept looking at them, then Blake said, "You both are lying, you both are trying to get to Quinn. Caden, why don't you go to Maya and ask her out?" Caden said, "I don't think so." Blake said, "Maya does like you, Caden." Caden said, "Why won't Maya talk to me? I tried to talk to her. Maya was with Quinn, and her friends went to them. I tried to talk with Maya, but Maya kept leaving, I know Maya doesn't like me." Pacey said, "Maya's shy. Maya has a crush on you." Caden was looking at them. Blake said, "Go to Maya, and ask Maya out." Caden was looking at Maya. Caden said, "I am too chicken to ask her out." Blake said, "Don't be, Go to her." Caden said, "What if Maya says no?" Pacey said, "I don't think so." Caden said, "Ok, I will try to ask Maya out." Trey said, "Go to Maya now." Caden was looking at them, Caden said, "You guys are going with me?" Trey said, "Why? Do you need us to ask her for you? We are not going to ask her for you." Caden said, "No, Ashely wants you, Trey and Taylor want Pacey. Right now, they ate looking at you both, and Blake wants to talk with Quinn." Blake said, "I don't know what I will say to her." Trey said, "Blake, go to Quinn." Blake ignored Trey, Blake said, "I think we better go with Caden. Caden is scared. Caden wants us to be with him when he asks Maya out." Caden said, "No, come on." Caden was walking away, the boys were making fun of Caden. Caden ignored them. Caden went to Maya, then sat with Maya, Maya looked at him, then the girls. Quinn and Taylor were grinning, Maya was quiet, and Pacey went to Taylor. Pacey was kissing Taylor, Trey was sitting with Ashely and was looking at Quinn, then Blake whispered "Blake, Quinn is waiting for you." Blake was looking at A-J. whispered, "Quinn wants you." Blake was quiet. A.J. said, "Go to her." Blake didn't speak. Blake looked at Quinn, then A.J. A.J. said, "You are chicken, like Caden." Blake said, "I am a chicken." AJ. said, "Oh, man." AJ. went to Quinn. A.J. and Quinn were talking. Blake kept looking at them. Blake was wondering what they were talking about. A.J. got up and said, "I'm going over to the woods, I will be back." They said, "Why are you going there?" A.J. said, "I lost my wallet in there." Caden said, "Do you need my help?" A.J. said, "No, stay there, and talk to Maya." Caden was quiet. A.J. smiled, then walked away. Ashely said, "I bet he went there to smoke a cigarette," Quinn said, "That's what I think." Blake said, "Smoke a cigarette? how do you know?" Ashely said, "We saw him." Blake was shocked. Blake said, "I didn't know that he smoked cigarettes." Emily said, "he's smoked for a few months." Caden said, "Why does A.J. smoke?" Emily said, "I don't know, but I think A.J.'s Cousin Cody gave A.J. Cigarettes." Parker said, "It's not good for A.J." Emily said, "I know, you talk with him about that." Parker said, "He won't talk with us about that. If we try to talk with him, you guys know his ways." Quinn said, "I know, but we have to keep doing that, He is our friend." Blake said, "Yeah." A,J. was walking in the woods, and was smoking a cigarette. All of a sudden, four men came up behind him and started to beat him up. A.J. was on the ground, screaming for help. A.J.'s Uncle Frank was chaperoning the boys and girls when he heard someone screaming for help. He started running to where the scream was coming from, then he found his nephew, his face was covered with blood. Everybody came, Quinn and Maya gasped. Caden said, "What happened?" Frank said, "I don't know, I found him here. Do you all have a phone with you guys?" Quinn said, "No, our phone won't work here." Frank sighed. Frank said, "Caden, go to my car, and use my phone." Frank gave Caden the key. Caden ran away, Frank tried to wake A.J. up, but Frank couldn't. Frank said, "A J. you are going to be okay. An ambulance is coming." Blake and Parker went to A.J. They were trying to help Frank wake up but they couldn't. Frank looked, Blake and Parker. Blake looked back at Frank, then Frank looked at A.J. Blake knew Frank was angry at them. Quinn, Ashley, and Emily at Frank. They knew that Frank was angry. Blake, Parker, and Frank tried to wake A-J. up, but they still couldn't. Taylor said, "Do you guys think A.J. will be ok?" Blake said, "I think he will be ok," Frank said, "I don't know." At same time, Frank was looking at Blake. Blake was quiet. Frank said, "What's taking Caden so long!" Blake said, "I don't know." Maya said, "What if someone got Caden?" Pacey said, "I don't think so." Maya said, 'Why is it taking Caden so long? I think you should go to Caden and see if Caden's ok." Pacey said, "Ok, I will be back." Pacey was ready to run away, but Taylor grabbed Pacey, Pacey looked at Taylor, and Pacey said, "I will be ok, I will be back." Taylor said, "Ok." Pacey kissed Taylor then Pacey ran away. Frank looked at Maya, then A.J. Blake looked back at Frank. Frank said, "A.J.?" A.J. did not wake up. They were waiting for Caden and Pacey for a few minutes. Finally, Caden and Pacey came back. Caden said, "They are on the way." Frank looked at Caden. Frank said, "ok." Frank looked at AJ. Frank said, "Caden, why did it take so long?" Caden said, "I was trying to get service, it's hard to get service here." Frank ignored him. Frank kept trying to wake up, but A.J. wouldn't wake up. They were waiting for the ambulance. Finally, the ambulance arrived, and took A.J. to the hospital.

Blake, Caden, Parker, Ashley, Trey, and Emily were sitting in the hobby room. They were waiting for Frank. Blake said, "Is Quinn, ok?" Emily said, "I think so, just shocked at what happened to A.J." Blake said, "I know, us too," Parker said, "I think Frank is mad at us." Emily said, "Why? We did not do anything to hurt him!" Parker said, "I know," Emily said, "We have to talk to him." Blake said, "Not now, let him get calmed down first." Trey said, "Blake is right." Emily was thinking about Frank and AJ. Trey said, "Emily, Frank and A.J. are going to be ok." Blake said, "You are right." Frank came. Frank said, "Go home, I don't want you all to be here!" Emily said, "Why? we just want to know if A.J. is ok." Frank said, "A.J. is going to be ok, but I don't want you all around A.J. anymore." Blake said, "What did we do?" Frank said, "You all let him go in the woods alone." Blake said, "We couldn't make A.J. stay with us." Frank said, "If A.J. wanted to go there, you all should have gone with A.J." Caden said, "Frank, you can't blame us for that. I asked him if he needed my help to find his wallet, and he said no." Frank said, "Caden, when I told you to go to the car, and get ambulance, why did it take you so long?" Caden said, "I told you about the Service. Frank said, "I think you are lying! You don't care about AJ. Maya don't care about him; Maya was not worried about AJ. Maya was worried about you." Caden said, "What?" Frank said, "When you went to my car, Maya was worried about you, Maya was scared that someone would hurt you, but why wasn't Maya worried about A.J.? Maya doesn't care about A.J. No one cared about him!" Frank was ready to walk away, but Caden grabbed Frank's arm. Caden said, "Get calm down, then talk to us." Frank hit Caden, Caden went to the floor. Blake pulled Frank away from Caden, Frank turned to Blake, Frank grabbed Blake's shirt, then pushed Blake to the wall. Blake groaned. Frank said, "Don't touch me!" Trey and Parker went to Frank. Trey said, "Don't!" Frank kept looking at Blake. Quinn, Taylor, Pacey, and Maya came. They looked at Frank. Frank pushed Blake to the wall again. Blake groaned. Frank said, "Don't try come to around us again." Frank was walking away. Quinn, Taylor, Maya, and Pacey went to them, Quinn said, "Are you ok?" Blake said, "I am ok." Quinn was looking at Caden. Quinn said, "Are you ok?" Caden said, "I am fine." Caden got up. Pacey said, "What's going on?" Emily explained what happened to them. Pacey said, "But it's not our fault. It's A.J. that was wanting to go to the woods. Caden asked him if he needed Caden's help. A.J. told him no." Caden said, "I know. We have to wait until Frank gets calm down, then we will try to talk with him again." Blake said, "I think the girls need to stay away from him." Caden said, "Yes, you are right." Trey said, "I think Frank is angry at Maya, too." Maya said, "What did I do?" Trey explained to Maya. Maya said, "Frank is wrong, I do care about A.J., he is our friend. I am going to talk with Frank." Caden said, "No, Maya. I don't want you to go to him. He is angry. Frank tried to hurt Blake." Maya looked at Caden, Quinn said, "Caden's right." Ashley said, "We better go, before Frank comes back." Pacey said, "Let's go." Maya whispered, "Caden, are you sure that you are okay?" Caden said, "I am fine." Maya looked at him, then Maya went to Quinn. Caden said, "Blake, I need to talk with you." Blake said, "What about?" Caden looked at his friends. Trey said, "We will be outside waiting for you both." Blake said, "Ok." Everyone walked away. Caden said, "Do you think Frank will try to hurt Maya?" Blake said, "I don't know. We have to watch Maya, and make sure Frank doesn't try to hurt Maya." Caden said, "Ok." Blake said, "Caden, Maya is ok. Don't worry." Caden said, "Ok. Frank is wrong, Maya does care about A.J." Blake said, "I know. Come on. They are waiting for us." Caden said, "Ok." They walked away. Frank came back. Frank was watching them. Frank was angry.

One Year Later

A.J.'s friends decided to go back to the cave and run camping. The girls went to the campsite and waited for the boys. Emily said, "We are going to have a great time." Quinn said, "We are." Emily said, "You will just stay with Blake all the time." Quinn smiled. Quinn said, "I love Blake, I know Blake is right for me." Taylor said, "We noticed that you both crazy for each other." Quinn said, "We are." Emily said, "What about Ryan?" Quinn said, "I don't love him anymore. Blake thought I was trying to make Blake jealous when I dated Ryan, but I wasn't, the boys told Blake that I was trying to make him jealous." Maya said, "We thought so too." Quinn said, "You all are wrong." Emily said, "Maya, when will you talk with Caden?" Maya said, "I don't know." Taylor said, "If Caden comes, you will talk to him?" Maya said, "Caden's coming?" Quinn said, "We don't know, but you need to talk with Caden about Erin. I know Caden didn't kiss her back." Maya said. "How do you know? You weren't there." Quinn said, "Taylor was there. Taylor told me everything." Maya looked at Taylor. Taylor said, "Caden didn't kiss her back when you saw them. After you walked away, Caden pushed Erin away, Caden told Erin he had a girlfriend. Caden loves you. Erin insulted you. Caden ignored here, and Caden walked away." Maya said, "You told me already but Erin came to me. Erin said that Erin and Caden went out. They kissed. They kissed a lot and they did talk bad about me." Taylor was laughing. Taylor said, "You know that Erin wants Caden so bad. Caden doesn't want her. Caden wants you.

When you left, I went to Caden. I told him about you. I am just scared. Did Ashley and Trey break up?" Quinn said, "Yeah, because Trey didn't want Ashley to leave but Ashley really wanted to go to that college." Maya saw Frank West coming. Maya said, "What is Frank doing here?" Taylor said, "Who?" Maya said, "Frank West." Frank interrupted. Frank said, "Hi, Girls." Emily, Quinn, and Taylor turned to him. They were shocked to see him. Frank said, "How are you all?" Quinn said, "We are doing great, how are you?" Frank said, "I am doing good. I know you guys must be puzzled as to why I am here." The girls were quiet. Frank said, "I don't want you guys to go there alone. I am scared someone will hurt you all like they did A.J." Maya said, "We will be fine. The four men are in jail now. They can't hurt us." Frank said, "I know but I still want to be with you all." Quinn said, "The boys will be with us. They won't let anything happen to us." Frank was getting ready to speak, but Blake interrupted. Blake said, "Hey." The girls and Frank looked at the boys. Blake said, "Frank, what are you doing here?" Pacey pulled Taylor to Pacey. Pacey held Taylor. He didn't want Frank to touch Taylor. Frank said, "I'm going to be with you guys to make sure you guys are okay." Blake said, "We are fine. We are adults. We don't need anyone to watch us." Frank looked at Blake. Blake said, "We want to be alone, without chaperoning." Frank said, "I know you don't want me to go with you buys because of what I did to you and Caden." Quinn looked at Blake. Quinn said, "Blake? What's he's talking about?" Blake looked at her then at Frank. Maya said, "What did you do to Caden?" Frank said, "You both don't know about that?" Maya said, "No." Blake said, "Frank, just forget it." Frank said, "I am trying to." Blake interrupted. Blake said, "When we get back, we will talk about that more." Frank was quiet. Blake said, "And, you are wrong. We do care about A.J." Frank said, "I know." Maya said, "How is A.J.? We haven't seen A.J. at school anymore." Frank said,

"It's a long story. I better go." Blake said, "Ok." Frank said, "Talk to you guys when you guys get back." Blake said, "Frank, I need to talk to you." Frank said, "Ok." Blake and Frank walked away from Blake's friends, where they can talk in private. Quinn kept looking at Blake. Maya said, "I wonder what he did to them?" Quinn kept looking at Blake. Maya said, "I wonder what he did to them?" Quinn said, "Me too. I am going to talk with Blake about that." Maya said, "Let me know what Blake says about Caden." Quinn said, "I will." Maya and Quinn looked at Frank. Maya said, "I don't want Frank to go with us." Quinn said, "Me either." Frank started walking away. Blake looked at Frank. Blake went to Quinn and Maya, Quinn said, "What did he do to you?" Blake said, "We will talk about that later." Quinn said, "Why not now? Blake looked at Quinn, Quinn said, "What did he do to you?" Blake said, "Ok. He went to my car and broke my car window." Quinn said, "That was him?" Blake said, "Yes. It was him." Quinn said, "Why you did not?" Blake interrupted. Blake said, "Because I didn't want you to worry, or go after him." Quinn said, "He needs to leave you alone." Blake said, "I know, has Frank come to you?" Quinn said, "Never." Blake kept looking at Quinn. Quinn said, "I'm not lying." Blake said, "Ok." Quinn and Blake kissed. Maya said, "What did Frank do to Caden?" Blake said, "Talk with Caden. Caden doesn't want anyone to know." Maya said, "Oh, ok." Emily, Taylor and Pacey came, Pacey said, "Everything ok?" Blake said, "Yeah, I won't let Frank go with us. I know he will try to do something to me or Caden." Pacey said, "I know." Maya was thinking about Caden. Maya whispered, "Caden's not coming." Emily looked at Maya. Emily said, "Where is Trey, Parker, and Caden?" Pacey said, "Trey and Ashley are arguing again, on the phone. Trey won't come here. Trey is trying to get Ashley back. Parker had to pick his things up, to get ready to move out, Caden should be here now. I guess Caden is late." Maya sighed. Pacey said, "You need to talk with

Caden. Caden didn't cheat on you with Erin." Taylor explained to Pacey what Maya told Taylor about Erin. Pacey said, "Erin's lying to you. Caden didn't go with her. Caden kept looking for you. I was with him all night. Caden was upset." Maya was quiet. Emily said, "Caden's here now." Maya looked at Emily. Maya turned and saw Caden. Maya looked away. Pacey said, "Talk with Caden. Caden did nothing wrong to you." Maya was quiet. Caden came. Caden said, "Sorry, I'm late." Blake said, "Us too. The girls got here first." Pacey said, "Guess who was here?" Caden said, "I don't know." Pacey said, "Frank West." Caden looked at Pacey, Caden said, "Everyone ok? Pacey said, "We are fine." Blake said, "This time Frank didn't try to hurt us or anything." Caden said, "Good. What was he doing here?" Blake explained everything to Caden, Caden said, "We don't need Frank to go with us. I know Frank will try to do something to us." Blake said, "That's what I think. I told him we don't need him." Caden said, "I'm glad that he didn't try to hurt you all." Blake said, "Me too. A.J. is in jail." Caden said, "Why? What did he do?" Blake said, "I don't know. Frank said it was a long story." Caden said, "I would like to go visit A.J., see how he is." Blake said, "I don't think it's a good idea, if you try to see A.J. again. Frank will go for you." Caden said, "I know." Maya was quiet and looked at Caden and Blake. Quinn said, "Maya, come on." Maya, Quinn, Emily, and Taylor were walking away from the boys. Quinn said, "Go to Caden, you need to talk with Caden about Erin. Try to work it out." Maya said, "No." Emily said, "Why not? I thought you really loved him." Maya said, "I do. I am scared." Quinn said, "Why are you scared?" Maya said, "What if we get back together again, and Erin keeps trying to get to Caden, to get Caden to change his mind about me?" Quinn said, "No, I know Caden won't. Caden really loves you." Maya said, "I don't know. Why hasn't he tried to talk to me? That means he doesn't love me." Caden interrupted and said, "You are wrong." Maya turned to Caden and said, "I love you with all my heart. I didn't try to talk to you because I wanted you to have a good time first. Then, I was going to try to talk with you." Caden started walking away. Maya looked at Caden, then the girls. Quin said, "We told you Caden loves you, not Erin. You need to stop talking to Erin." Maya said, "Erin kept coming up to me." Quinn said, "Because Erin was trying to get to you to not Caden again." Pacey said, "Girls, we are ready to go. We need to go before it gets dark." Taylor said, "Ok, we are coming." They went to the boys. Caden looked at Maya. Caden was quiet. Maya caught Caden looking at her. Caden looked away. Maya looking at Caden, Emily said, "Maya, come on." Maya looked at Emily, then Maya went to Emily. Blake went to Caden, Blake said, "You need to talk with Maya tonight." Caden said, "You think she will talk with me? I don't think so. Maya thinks I want Erin." Blake said, "Talk to Maya about it, I think Maya will talk with you. The girls are trying to get her to talk to you." Caden looked at Maya again. Pacey said, "Come on."

They were walking up the hill for one hour. Taylor was panting. Blake looked around, then at Taylor. Pacey said, "Are you ok?" Taylor said, "I'm fine." Blake said, "Let's stay here for a night." Quinn said, "We can have a break now." Quinn put her backpack on the ground. Blake went to Quinn and kissed her. They took a rest for a while. Then they put their tent up. Caden and Blake started a campfire. Taylor was taking a walk in the woods. Pacey went to look for Taylor, Taylor didn't know that Pacey was looking for her. Pacey found Taylor. Pacey went to Taylor. Taylor turned. Taylor gasped. Taylor said, "Oh, Pacey, you scared me." Pacey said, "Oh, I'm sorry, but I don't want you to be alone in the woods, you know better." Taylor said, "Sorry, I wasn't thinking about that." Pacey sighed, Pacey pulled Taylor to him, Taylor said, "No one's going to try to hurt me." Pacey said, "I know, but you never know, those four men hurt A.J." Taylor was quiet. Pacey said, "I don't want you to be alone in the woods. If you want to go for a walk, ask me to go with you." Taylor said, "Ok." Pacey said, "I don't want anything to happen to you." Pacey kissed Taylor, Pacey said, "I can't wait to get married." Taylor smiled. Taylor said, "Me either." They kissed again. Pacey said, "I love you." Taylor smiled. Taylor said, "I love you too." Pacey said, "Come on." They went to their friends. Quinn said, "Taylor, I thought you ran away from us." Taylor said, "No, I wanted to walk around, but Pacey made me come back here." Quinn said, "You know it's a bad idea for you to go out there alone." Taylor said, "I know, I wasn't thinking about that." Blake said, "Quinn, we need to talk." Quinn said, "Ok." Quinn got up. Quinn and Blake walked away. Quinn said, "Is everything ok?" Blake said, "Yes, I just need to get Maya and Caden to talk." Quinn said, "They will, look at Maya." They looked over at Maya, and she kept looking over at Caden. Quinn said, "Taylor kept trying to tell Maya about that, I guess Maya knows Erin lied to her now." Blake said, "If Maya still won't, we have to do something." Quinn said, "Emily, Taylor and I have a plan." Blake said, "Good, let me know." Quinn said, "I will." They looked back over at Maya again. Maya was looking around. Caden was watching Maya. Pacey went to Caden. Pacey said, "Go to Maya." Caden said, "Maya won't," Pacey said, "Try to talk with her." Caden said, "Ok."

Caden went to Maya. Caden said, "Maya, we need to talk." Maya looked at Caden. Maya said, "What about?" Caden said, "About us." Maya said, "Not now. Later. I want to go to sleep. I'm very tired." Caden said, "I know you don't want to talk with me. You are lying. You are not tired." Maya said, "I am tired." Maya was ready to walk away from Caden, but Caden grabbed Maya. Caden said, "You are lying. You don't want to talk with me. You are trying to avoid me." Maya said, "No, I am not trying to avoid you." Caden said, "Then, why wouldn't you talk to me all day?" Maya said, "Because I don't know what to say to you." Caden said, "You're lying." Maya said, "Whatever." Maya was ready to walk to her tent, but Caden stopped Maya, Caden said, "I love you." Maya looked at Caden. Caden said, "Do you love me?" Maya said, "I do but." Caden interrupted. Caden said, "You don't need to let Erin get to you. You know Erin wants me but I don't want her. I want you." Maya said, "I don't want to talk about Erin tonight, we will talk about that tomorrow. I am very tired. I am going to sleep." Maya got free, then Maya started walking away. Caden said, "Maya!" Maya ignored him. Maya went to her tent. Emily said, "Maya's scared. I'll talk to her for you." Emily went to her. Caden was quiet. Caden looked at Maya's tent. Pacey said, "Just give her time. Maya will talk with you soon." Caden said, "I don't think so. I think she doesn't love me anymore." Pacey said, "She does. She is just scared that she will get hurt again." Caden said, "I am not going to try to hurt her." Pacey said, "I know, it's Erin. Erin will try to do anything to hurt her." Caden sighed. Caden said, "How can I get Erin to leave me alone?" Pacey said, "You need to tell her that you don't want her." Caden said, "I've told her many times. Erin won't let me go." Pacey said, "Keep trying to talk with Erin." Caden said, "No. If I talk with Erin, Maya will think I'm trying to get with Erin." Pacey said, "You are right. I will ask Taylor to explain to Maya that you have to talk with Erin." Caden said, "Ok." Pacey said, "Maya is scared that if she gets you back, Erin will steal you from her. Maya just doesn't want to get hurt again." Caden said, "I am not going to let Erin hurt Maya." Pacey said, "I know. Maya will talk with you soon." Caden was quiet. Pacey said, "I am going to talk with Taylor." Caden said, "Ok." Pacey walked away. Caden looked at Maya's tent. Someone was watching everyone. They didn't know that someone was watching them.

Emily was cooking breakfast for them. Quinn and Taylor came in. Quinn said, "It smells good." Emily looked at them and smiled. Pacey came in. Pacey looked at Emily. Pacey said, "I didn't know you could cook." Taylor said, "Oh, we love her cooking. She is very good." Quinn said, "I know you will love her cooking." Pacey said, "What if Emily." Taylor interrupted. Taylor pushed Pacey. Taylor said, "Don't try and make a joke." Pacey laughed. Pacey pulled Taylor to him and kissed her. Pacey said, "Emily knows I'm just joking." Emily said, "Yeah, I know." Taylor said, "Good." Caden and Blake came in. Caden said, "Good morning." They looked at Caden and Blake. Blake said, "Something smells good." Caden said, "Yeah." Caden looked around. Emily said, "If you are looking for Maya, Maya is still in the tent asleep." Caden said, "Oh." Emily said, "Maya was up talking about you and Erin all night. That's why she's still asleep." Caden sighed. Caden said, "What did Maya say about me and Erin?" Emily said, "I can't say." Caden said, "Ok, then I'm going to talk with Maya later." Emily said, "Caden, Maya really does love you." Caden said, "I love her, with my all heart. I've been trying to talk with Maya about Erin. I want Maya to know that I don't want Erin. I want Maya." Emily said, "I think she will talk with you soon, Caden. Just give her time." Caden got quiet. Emily said, "You will get Maya back." Caden said, "You think so?" Emily said, "I know you will get her back." Caden said, "I am going to give her some time." Emily said, "Good." Caden sat on the ground, Quinn said, "I am going to." Maya interrupted. Maya said, "Good morning." Everyone looked over at Maya. Emily said, "Good morning." Caden got up, Caden said, "I'm gonna go change clothes!" Caden walked away. Maya looked around, then at

Caden. Taylor over to Maya, Taylor started whispering to Maya. No one could hear them. Maya was quiet. Emily said, "Breakfast is ready." Pacey said, "gonna go let Caden know breakfast is ready." Maya said, "Let me." Pacey said, "Ok." Maya walked away. Quinn said, "I think Maya is going to talk with Caden." Blake said, "I think so." Blake looked at Quinn and kissed her. Blake said, "I love you." Quinn said, "I love you, too." Blake held Quinn tight.

Maya said, "Caden?" Caden got out of the tent, Caden looked at Maya. Maya said, "Breakfast is ready." Caden said, "Thanks, but I'm not hungry." Maya said, "I know you are hungry; you just don't want to bother me." Caden said, "I will be fine." Maya looked at Caden. Maya said, "We do need to talk." Caden said, "Yeah, we do." Maya said, "You know I love you. I am scared Erin will try to steal you from me. I know Erin won't let you go." Caden interrupted. Caden said, "I don't want her, I want you." Maya interrupted. Maya said, "I'm sorry," Caden looked at Maya and smiled. Caden pulled Maya to him and kissed her. Caden said, "I'm sorry too." Maya kissed Caden back. Caden said, "I've missed you." Maya said, "I've missed you too." They kissed again. Maya said, "Don't let Erin." Caden interrupted, Caden said, "Forget her, kiss me." Maya smiled. They kissed again. Quinn, Emily, and Taylor were excited. Quinn said, "Finally!" Caden and Maya looked at them. Taylor said, "Now don't let Erin win." Caden said, "Erin won't. Maya is mine" Maya looked at Caden again. Caden said, "I love you; I won't let Erin ruin us again." Maya said, "You better not." Caden kissed Maya. Emily said, "I guess we better let them be." Taylor said, "Come on." The girls went to Pacey and Blake. Quinn said, "They are kissing." Blake said, Taylor said, "Caden and Maya are kissing now!" Blake said, "Finally! how?" Emily said, "They were talking, then kissing." Pacey said, "You three were spying on them?"

Quinn smiled. Blake laughed. Maya and Caden came over. Blake said, "I heard that you two are back together again." Caden said, "Yeah, we are." Caden smiled at Maya. Caden said, "I'm not letting you go." Maya said, "That's good," Maya smiled, then kissed Caden. Blake said, "Caden, Maya, you both can wait, we have to go." Caden said, "Ok, I'm going to pack my stuff," Maya said, "No, you are not, you have to eat first. We are hungry." Caden said, "I am not." Maya said, "You have not eaten." Caden said, "If it makes you happy, I will eat." Maya smiled. Blake said, "You two go eat. We going to pack our stuff." Maya said, "Ok." They walked away.

They were walking in the hills. After walking a long trail. Taylor had to stop. She couldn't hardly breathe. Blake looked at Taylor. Blake said, "Are you ok?" Taylor said, "I'm ok, I'm just not used to walking in the woods for long." Pacey said, "Let's take a break." Blake said, "Yeah." Blake was looking for mound. Quinn said, "Blake, let's stay here, I like it here." Blake said, "Me too." Quinn smiled at Blake. Blake said, "We are going to stay here." Taylor said, "You guys don't have to stay because of me." Quinn said, "No, I like it here. It's so beautiful, and you need to get a rest too." Pacey said, "Yeah." Taylor said, "OK." Blake said, "Quinn, come on. Let's look around." Quinn said, "Ok." They walked away. Taylor was sitting on the ground. Pacey went to Taylor, Pacey said, "Are you ok?" Taylor smiled at Pacey, Taylor said, "I will be ok," Pacey said, "Good." Pacey's arm was around Taylor's shoulder. Caden grabbed Maya, and Maya gasped. Caden pulled Maya to him and kissed her. Taylor, Pacey, and Emily were looking at them. Emily, Taylor, and Pacey looked at each other and laughed. Caden and Maya looked over at them. Caden said, "What?" Pacey said, "Nothing." Caden said, "Come on." Maya said, "Ignore them." Caden said, "Yeah." Pacey said, "Caden, come on." Pacey got up, and Caden said, "Maya, I will be back." Maya said, "Ok." Caden gave Maya a kiss, then he and Pacey walked away. Emily and Taylor looked over at Maya. Taylor said, "We are so happy for you, Maya." Maya smiled. Maya said, "Thank you." Maya went over to them, they did not know someone was watching them. The girls were talking about Caden. Taylor said, "I am so happy that you both are together again." Maya smiled. Maya said, "Me too, we talked about Erin. Caden said that he tried to talk with Erin about me. Caden doesn't want Erin, Caden wants but Erin won't let Caden go." Taylor said, "I am going to talk with Erin." Maya said, "You don't have to. I am going to talk with her." Taylor said, "I'll go with you." Emily said, "Yeah we will go with you." Maya smiled at them. Maya said, "You both are my best friends. I don't know what to do." Creak noises interrupted them, Maya stopped speaking because they heard some noises. They were looking around, Maya said, "Did you hear that?" Taylor said, "I think it was Blake and Quinn." Maya said, "Maybe, I think we better go to Caden and Pacey." Taylor said, "Why?" Maya said, "You never know it might not be Blake and Quinn." Emily said, "I think Maya's right." Taylor said, "Ok." But Caden and Pacey came back before they left. They scared the girls. The girls gasped. Caden said, "Are you three, okay?" Emily said, "We are ok. You just scared us." Taylor explained everything to them. Caden said, "It's Blake and Quinn." Maya said, "How do you know? What if it's not them?" Caden said, "I am going to check. Where did you hear the noises?" Emily, Taylor and Maya pointed over to the woods. Caden said, "I will be back." Maya said, "Be careful!" Caden said, "I will." Caden started walking away. Maya kept looking at Caden. Pacey said, "Caden will be fine." Maya was quiet and looked at Pacey. Caden was walking around, but Caden couldn't find Blake and Quinn. Caden said, "Blake! Quinn!" They did not answer him back. Caden turned. He saw a raccoon,

Caden started laughing. Caden thought that the noises the girls heard were from the raccoon. Caden went back to Maya, Emily, Pacey, Blake, and Quinn. Blake said, "Everything is Ok?" Caden said, "Everything is great, I think the noises they heard were coming from a raccoon." Maya looked at Caden, Maya knew it was not a raccoon. Maya said, "What if it's not a raccoon?" Caden said, "I saw a raccoon, there is no one out there." Maya had a funny feeling about it. Caden said, "Maya, don't worry. I didn't see anyone there, just a raccoon." Maya said, "Ok." Caden went to Maya. Caden said, "Everything is great, there is no one there. If you are worried about the men who beat A.J., They are in jail. They will not be here to try to hurt us again." Maya said, "Ok, I guess I just panicked," Caden kissed Maya, Caden said, "You are going to be ok." Blake said, "Let's not talk about A.J. and those men." Caden said, "Ok." Blake said, "Let's make a fire. It's getting dark." Pacey said, "Let's do it." Pacey and Blake started a campfire. Maya, Quinn, Emily, and Taylor were talking. Caden was looking at Maya. Quinn said, "Hey, let's play games." Pacey said, "What kind?" Emily said, "Truth or Dare" Pacey said, "I hate that game." Taylor said, "Or you are scared." Pacey said, "I am not." Taylor said, "Maybe you are hiding from me." Pacey said, "No." Taylor said, "Why don't you want to play?" Pacey said, "Let's play." Quinn said, "Great! Maya, you first." Maya said, "Caden, Truth or Dare?" Caden said, "Truth." Maya said, "Are you happy that you came here with us?" Caden said, "I am very happy because I got you back." Maya smiled. Maya said, "It's your turn, Quinn." Quinn said, "Taylor?" Taylor said, "Truth." Quinn said, "Are you ready to get married?" Taylor smiled. Taylor said, "Yes, I am ready to get married." Caden said, "It's my turn, Maya?" Maya looked at Caden, Caden said, "Truth or Dare?" Maya said, "Truth." Caden said, "I was hoping it was Dare." Maya smiled. Maya said,

"Why?" Caden said, "Nothing, are you happy that we are together?" Maya said, "Yep, I am," Caden smiled. Caden kissed Maya.

They were playing games. Someone was watching them.

Everyone went to sleep, but Caden, Maya, Blake, and Quinn. They stayed up talking. Blake said, "I will be right back. I am going to get a drink." Quinn said, "Ok." Blake said, "Do you want me to get you guys anything?" Quinn said, "No, thanks." Maya said, "Thanks." Blake said, "OK." Blake walked away. Maya said, "Caden, I want to ask you something about Frank." Caden said, "What about him?" Maya said, "When Frank came back, Frank wanted to go with us. Blake told him that we didn't need him, he said We didn't want him to go with us because he did something to you and Blake. What did he do to you?" Caden said, "I don't want to talk about him." Maya said, "I want to know." Caden looked at Maya. Quinn said, "Forget Frank." Maya said, "Quinn, do you know what happened?" Quinn said, "No, I just don't want to talk about Frank." Blake came back, Blake said, "What about Frank?" Blake sat down with Quinn, then opened a Pepsi. Quinn said, "Maya wanted to know what did he do to Caden." Blake looked at Caden. Caden mouthed to Blake, "Don't." Maya said, "Why do you guys do not want me to know?" Caden said, "We don't want to talk about Frank." Maya said, "Did Frank hurt you?" Caden said, "No." Maya Said, "Blake." Blake looked over at Maya. Maya said, "Did Frank hurt Caden?" Blake looked back at Caden, then Maya. Blake said, "Frank just kept bothering him." Maya kept looking at Blake. Caden said, "Maya, Frank blamed me for not going with A.J." Maya said, "But you asked A.J. If he wanted you to go with him, and he told you no." Caden said, "I know." Blake said, "He told Caden that he should've ignored him, and went with him anyways. Frank kept trying to fight with him, one time he tried to stab Caden with..." Caden interrupted, Caden said, "Let's not talk about that." Maya said, "Caden, he tried to stab you with a knife?" Caden said, "He tried, but Blake stopped him." Maya said, "Why didn't you." Caden interrupted. Caden said, "Because we don't want you or Quinn to worry about us, Frank kept coming to us." Blake said, "That's why I didn't want Frank to come with us, I was afraid that he would try to hurt us." Quinn said, "Let's not talk about Frank!" Blake said, "Quinn, if Frank comes around you, will you let me know?" Quinn said, "I will, but Frank never did try to come to me." Caden said, "You never know, Maya, you need to let me know too" Maya said, "Ok." Blake said, "When we get back, what are you going to do about Erin, Caden?" Caden sighed, Caden said, "I don't know. I need someone to talk to her and tell her to let me go. I don't want Erin. I want Maya. I love Maya." Maya said, "I love you too. We have to do something about Erin." Caden said, "No, I'm going to try to find someone to talk with her for us. I don't want you to talk to Erin again. Erin will lie to you, and you will listen to her, I don't want to lose you again." Maya said, "This time I'm not going to listen her." Caden looked at Maya. Caden knew that Maya would listen to Erin because it's happened to them a few times. Caden said, "You better not." Maya said, "I won't." Caden said, "Ok." Quinn said, "I think it's a good idea to let someone talk with her for you both," Maya said, "Ok." Maya looked at Caden. Caden said, "I love you." Maya smiled. Maya said, "I love you, too." They kissed. Blake said, "I know you both are going to be ok." Caden said, "You are right, Blake." Maya was quiet. Quinn said, "They are right. You both are going to be ok." Maya said, "I know," Caden pulled her to him, and held her tight, Caden whispered, "We are going to be ok." Maya said, "I know." Caden kissed Maya again. Blake said, "When we get back, what are you going to do, Caden?" Caden said, "Get ready for college, and get a job, what about you?" Blake said, "Me too, and I am looking for an apartment. Caden, do you want to live with me? We can pay half of the bills." Caden said, "Good idea." Maya was quiet. Blake, Quinn and Caden were talking. Caden looked at Maya. Maya was still quiet. Maya was thinking. Caden said, "Maya?" Maya looked at Caden, Caden said, "Are you okay?" Maya said, "Yes, why? Caden said, "You are being quiet." Maya said, "I am tired." Caden kept looking at Maya. Maya said, "Oh. I was thinking about Frank. I am scared that when we get back, Frank will try to hurt you again, Caden." Caden said, "Don't worry. Frank won't know where we are. When we're going to college, we won't see Frank again." Maya looked at Caden. Caden said, "Forget him." Maya said, "I am trying, but I am worried." Blake said, "Don't, everything will be ok, Frank won't know where we are when we go to college." Quinn said, "What if Frank's following you both?" Blake said, "We will call the police if we find out he is." Quinn said, "Ok." Maya said, "When Frank tried to hurt you, Caden, did you report it to the police?" Caden said, "I did. Let's not talk about Frank again. Forget Frank." Maya said, "I can't, I am worried about you." Caden said, "Don't worry about me. I will be fine, but I am worried about you, I am afraid that Frank will try to hurt you." Maya said, "Frank never has tried to come around me or talk to me." Caden looked at Maya. Caden said, "I know how to get you to forget about Frank." Maya looked at Caden, Maya said, "You can't." Caden said, "I will try." Caden smiled. Maya knew what Caden was trying to do. Maya said, "Don't." Caden grabbed her and started tickling her. Maya laughed. Caden kept tickling her. Maya cried and pushed him away, but she couldn't. So, Maya decided to pull him to her, and kiss him. Caden stopped tickling her. Maya pulled Caden to her, Caden was ready to speak, but Maya interrupted him. Maya started kissing him, Quinn was looking at them, Quinn whispered, "Blake, do you think you two will be ok?" Blake whispered, "We will be fine, Frank won't come around, "Quinn said, "Ok." Blake pulled Quinn to him and held him tight.

They were hiking again. Maya yawned. Emily said, "You didn't sleep well?" Maya said, "I stayed up all night." Emily said, "With Caden?" Maya said, "Yeah with Caden, Quinn, and Blake. You were tired and went to sleep early." Emily said, "Yeah, I was worn out." Maya said, "I know." Maya was quiet. Emily looked at Maya, Emily knew something was wrong. Emily said, are you ok?" Maya said, "I'm ok, just very tired." Emily said, "I don't think you are ok. I can tell something is wrong." Maya was looking at Caden. Caden didn't know that Maya was looking at him. Caden was talking with Pacey. Maya whispered, "I am worried about Caden." Emily said, "If you are worried about Erin and Caden, Don't, Caden won't." Caden heard Emily. Maya knew that Caden heard Emily, Maya looked at Caden, then Emily. Maya said, "No, It's not about Erin." Emily looked at Caden, then Maya. Emily whispered, "Sorry." Caden looked back at Emily and then Maya. Maya caught Caden looking at her and smiled. Caden smiled back. Caden mouthed to Maya, "Stop worrying about Erin." Maya mouthed, "I'm not." Caden mouthed to her, "We will talk, later." Emily said, "Maya." Maya looked at Emily. Emily said, "Why are you worried about Caden?" Maya whispered, "I am afraid that Frank will come back and try to hurt Caden again." Emily whispered, "Again?" Maya whispered, "I'll tell you later." Emily said, "Ok." Emily was looking around, Emily whispered, "Did Frank hurt Caden?" Maya whispered, "Blake and Caden said that Frank tried to stab Caden. I think that Frank hurt him." Emily was shocked that Frank tried to stab Caden.

They were whispering to each other. Caden was looking at them. Caden was wondering what they were talking about. Pacey said, "Are you ok?" Caden said, "I am fine, I'm just wondering what Maya and Emily are talking about. I heard them. Maya's worried about me." Pacey said, "I heard them. too." Caden said, "Maya doesn't need to worry about me and Erin. I don't want Erin." Pacey said, "I know. You have to talk with Maya about that again," Caden said, "I will." Emily said, "Why didn't he go to the police?" Maya said, "Caden said that he did." Emily said, "No one knows about that." Maya said, "I know." Caden pulled Maya to him, Caden whispered, "You need to stop worrying about me and Erin," Maya said, "I am not." Caden said, "I heard Emily." Maya said, "I told her that I'm worried about you. She thought it was about Erin, but I am not worried about Erin." Caden said. "What you are worried about?" Maya said, "Frank will try to hurt you" Caden sighed. Caden said, "Forget him. I want us to have a good time and not think about Frank." Maya said, "I know, I am trying not to think about Frank, but I can't." Blake said, "Hey!" They looked at Blake. Blake said, "There's a Pond." Caden said, "Come on, Maya." Maya and Caden went to Blake, Pacey, Taylor, and Quinn. Quinn said, "We are going to swim." Maya said, "I am going to rest." Caden looked at Maya. Maya put her bags on the ground, Blake took his shirt off, then went into the pond. Blake said, "Oh, it's so cold, but it feels good." Quinn, Taylor, Emily, and Pacey went into the pond. They were swimming. Caden looked at them, then at Maya. Caden was smiling, Caden looked at Blake, Taylor, Pacey, Quinn, and Emily again. They knew that Caden was going to throw Maya in the pond. Maya was ready to sit on the ground, but Caden grabbed her, and Maya gasped. Maya said, "Don't!" Caden wouldn't listen to her. Caden pulled Maya to the pond, then threw her into the pond. Maya gasped. Maya said, "It's so cold!" Caden was laughing. Maya said, "Caden! You are going to get paid back!" Caden said, "Nah." Caden jumped in the pond. Maya went to Caden. They were swimming for a while. Quinn said, "I am getting out.

I am so cold." Maya said, "Me too." Blake said, "Come on, stay with me, Quinn." Quinn said, "No, I am too cold." Blake was ready to grab Quinn, Blake was trying to make Quinn stay with Blake, but Quinn got away from Blake, Quinn said, "I will be back." Blake said, "Ok." The girls got out of the pond. They went to the ground. They were talking. Blake, Pacey, and Caden were talking. Emily said, "I wonder why Parker is leaving? I thought Parker was going with us to college." Quinn said, "Me too." Taylor said, "He's leaving because Of Quinn." Quinn said, "Yeah, right." Emily said, "What did Quinn do to Parker?" Taylor said, "Parker had a crush on Quinn, but Parker couldn't do that to Blake, so it's hard for him to watch them. He wants to leave. He doesn't want to bother you guys." Quinn said, "No." Maya interrupted, Maya said, "I noticed that Parker kept watching Quinn. I didn't know that Parker had a crush on Quinn," Quinn kept looking at Taylor. Quinn said, "Are you kidding?" Taylor said, "No, Blake knew." Quinn said, "What?" Taylor said, "He doesn't want you to know. He's afraid that he will lose you. Blake's really crazy about you." Quinn said, "I don't want Parker, I am crazy about Blake. Blake knows that I love him." Taylor said, "I know you do love Blake, but Blake was afraid, that's all. Parker told Blake that he didn't want to steal you from him. Parker had to leave." Quinn kept looking at the girls. Quinn said, "No way." Taylor said, "Ask Blake." Quinn said, "I will, If Parker does have a crush on me, I am not going to dare him, I'm going to stay with Blake." Maya said, "I know." Quinn said, "I love Blake so much." Blake said, "I love you so much too." Quinn turned to Blake; Blake was sitting with Quinn. Quinn said, "You heard everything?" Blake said, "I heard you say that you love me so much, that's all." Quinn was quiet. Blake said, "Is everything ok?" Quinn said, "Everything is fine." Blake said, "You're acting like you didn't want me to hear everything. What were you guys talking about." Quinn said, "We will talk about that later." Blake said, "Ok." Caden went to Maya, Caden said, "Maya, you should stay and swim with me." Maya said, "No, it was cold." Caden pulled Maya to him, and Maya yawned. Caden looked at Maya, Caden said, "Are you tired?" Maya said, "I didn't sleep well. I stayed up with you guys all night." Caden said, "Why don't you go to sleep now, I'm going to set up the tent for you." Maya said, "I can do it." Caden said, "Stay and rest. Pacey, help me." Pacey said, "Ok." Pacey and Caden got up, and Caden grabbed Maya's bag. Caden and Pacey were walking away. Maya was looking at Caden. Quinn said, "Blake, we need to talk." Blake looked at Quinn. Blake said, "Ok." Quinn said, "Come on." Quinn and Blake got up, then they walked away. Maya said, "Taylor, are you kidding about Parker?" Taylor said, "No, Parker's in love with Quinn." Blake said, "Is everything ok?" Quinn said, "You know about Parker?" Blake said, "What about him?" Quinn said, "He's leaving because of me." Blake looked at her, Blake said, "How do you know?" Quinn said, "Taylor told me." Blake Said, "Oh, He had a crush on you." Quinn said, "I had no idea, why didn't you tell me?" Blake said, "Because I was afraid that you would leave me for him. I don't want to lose you. I love you." Quinn said, "You are not going to lose me. I'm not going to leave you for him, I love you." Blake said, "What if you change your mind about us." Quinn interrupted, Quinn said, "It will not happen, I want you, only you, not Parker or any other guy." Blake looked at Quinn. Quinn said, "Why would you think that?" Blake looked away. Blake said, "I saw you two. You were picking each other a lot, and you looked like you like him a lot." Quinn said, "I love him as a brother. We were playing, that's all. That doesn't mean I am in love with him. I am in love with you, not him." Blake was looking at her. Quinn said, "I would never date him. He's been my friend since kindergarten. I don't have any feelings for him." Blake kept looking at Quinn. Quinn came closer to Blake, Quinn said, "You don't need to worry about that." Quinn kissed him. Quinn was ready to walk away, but Blake wouldn't let her go. Blake held her tight. Blake said, "I don't know what I would do if I lost you. I love you." Quinn said, "You are not going lose me." Blake said, "That's good." Blake kissed her, someone was watching them. Someone was walking around who kept on watching them. Blake whispered something to Quinn. Quinn smiled. Quinn was ready to kiss him, but Quinn stopped and looked over to the woods. Blake turned, and looked around, then turned to Quinn, Blake said, "What's wrong?" Quinn said, "I think I saw someone there." Blake said, "Where?" Quinn pointed over to the woods. Blake kept looking around. Blake said, "I don't see anyone there." Blake was ready to walk, but Quinn stopped him, Quinn "Where are you going?" Blake said, "I'm going over there to see if someone is there." Quinn said, "I don't want you to go there alone." Blake was looking at Quinn. Blake Said, "Ok, Caden!" Quinn said, "You are going to send him? Blake said, "No, I am going to ask him to go with me to check." Quinn said, "But don't want you to go out there, what if someone is waiting for you there." Blake interrupted. Blake said, "I don't think someone is waiting for us." Quinn was quiet. Blake said, "I am going to be fine."

Caden came. Blake explained to Caden what Quinn saw. Caden said, "Oh." Blake said, "Can you go with me to check?" Caden said, "I can." Blake said, "Quinn, we will be back, go to Pacey, Taylor, and Maya." Quinn said, "Blake." Blake interrupted, Blake said, "We will be fine." Quinn said, "Ok." Quinn was walking away. Blake said, "Come on, Caden." Caden and Blake started walking over in the woods. Caden said, "Taylor said that Quinn knew about Parker." Blake said, "Taylor told Quinn." Caden said, "I know, Maya told me. What did Quinn say?" Blake told him what happened, Caden said, "I'm glad that everything is ok."

Blake said, "Me too, I was scared." Caden said, "I know how you feel. Caden was looking around. Caden said, "There is no one here." Blake said, "I know." Caden was walking around and wasn't looking. He didn't see the drop off and fell down the mountain and started rolling. Blake said, "Caden!" Blake ran and looked down, Caden had hit the ground, and fainted. Blake Said, "Caden!" Caden didn't wake up. Blake said, "Pacey! I need your help!" Blake went down to Caden. Blake tried to wake him up, but Caden wouldn't wake up. Blake said, "Caden?" Pacey, Taylor, Quinn, Emily, and Maya came. They looked down at Blake, and Caden. Maya said, "Caden!" Maya was ready to go down, but Pacey stopped Maya. Pacey said, "Let me." Maya interrupted. Maya said, "I'm going to him, you're not going to stop me." Pacey said, "Ok, I'm going with you, come on," Blake said, "Maya's coming, I know you don't want her to see you like this, wake up, Caden." Maya and Pacey went down to Caden and Blake. Maya went to Caden, Maya said, "Caden?" Pacey said, "What happened?" Blake explained what had happened to them. Maya Said, "Caden, wake up." Pacey said, "He's ok." Maya said, "How do you know?" Pacey was looking at Maya, Pacey said, "My mom's a doctor, she taught me a lot, and I'm going to college to become a doctor." Maya was looking at Caden. Finally, Pacey got Caden to wake up. Caden groaned. Maya said, "Caden?" Caden was looking at Maya. Maya said, "Are you ok?" Caden said, "I'm fine." Caden tried to sit up, but Pacey stopped him, Pacey said, "Not too fast." Caden looked at Pacey, Caden said, "Doctor, I'm fine." Pacey said, "I know how you are." Caden wouldn't listen to Pacey, and tried to get up, but Pacey and Blake stopped him. Caden groaned. Maya said, "Caden?" Caden said, "It's my shoulder." Emily said, "Is Caden okay?" Everyone was looking at Taylor, Quinn, and Emily. Caden said, "I'm fine." Maya said, "Don't lie." Caden said, "I'm not lying, it's just my shoulder, I'm going to be ok." Caden was ready to sit up,

Pacey said, "Caden." Caden said, "I need to sit up." Pacey said, "Ok, we are going take you to the hospital, and make sure you are." Caden said, "No, I'm fine." Blake said, "I think we better take you." Caden said, "I'm fine, I don't need to see a doctor." Maya said, "You do need to see the doctor, you were unconscious." Caden said, "I know, but I am going to be fine." Maya was looking at Caden. Blake looked at Pacey, Pacey Said, "Ok, Caden, you can't go to sleep for two hours, we have to watch you." Caden said, "But I am fine." Pacey said, "I know, come on." Pacey and Blake helped Caden up. Caden groaned, Caden touched his shoulder. Maya said, "Pacey, what if it's broken?" Pacey Said, "Caden, let me look at your shoulder." Caden said, "Ok." Caden was looking at Maya. Maya was watching them. Caden said, "I am fine, Maya." Pacey said, "Maya, I don't think it's broken. Caden can move his shoulder." Maya said, "Good." Caden said, "Let's go."

Caden was sitting on the ground. Pacey and Taylor were whispering to each other. Maya, Quinn, and Emily were talking, but Maya kept looking at Caden. Quinn said, "Maya, Caden's going to be ok." Maya said, "I know, but can't help it. I'm worried about him." Emily said, "Go talk to him." Maya Said, "I will be back." Quinn said, "Ok." Maya was walking away. Emily said, "Maya worries too much." Quinn said, "I know because Maya loves Caden so much." Emily said, "You are right" Emily and Quinn were looking at them. Blake came over. Blake said, "Hey." They looked at Blake. Blake said, "What's up?" Quinn said, "Nothing. We were talking about Maya." Blake said, "Oh!" Blake held Quinn tight. Blake was looking at Caden and Maya. Blake said, "I guess Maya's worried about Caden?" Quinn said, "You are right," Blake said, "Caden's going to be ok." Quinn said, "I know." Blake said, "What do you guys want to do?" Quinn said, "I don't know." Blake was looking around, Blake said, "Want to go swimming again?" Quinn said, "Right now?" Blake said, "Why not?" Quinn said, "It's too cold." Blake said, "I will keep you warm." Quinn said, "No way. I'm not going swimming tonight." Blake said, "It'll be fun. Come on, swim with us." Quinn was looking at Blake. Blake said, "Em?" Emily said, "I'm going to go change, I will be back." Emily was walking away. Blake kept looking at Quinn. Quinn sighed. Quinn said, "Ok." Blake smiled. Blake said, "We are going to have a great time." Quinn said, "You guys will, but I don't know if I will have a great time because it's too cold." Blake said, "I know you will have a great time." Blake kissed Quinn. Blake said, "Go and change, I will wait for you there." Quinn sighed again. Quinn said, "Ok." Quinn walked away, Blake said, "Maya, Caden." They looked over at him. Blake said, "We are going to go swimming, want to join us?" Maya said, "Right now? It's too cold." Blake said, "If we play around, it will keep us warm." Caden said, "Blake's right. Maya wants to go swimming?" Maya said, "You are going to swim?" Caden said, "If you want to, I'll go with you." Maya knew that Caden wanted to go, Maya said, "Ok." Blake said, "Great, we will see you guys there." Blake was walking away. Maya said, "Caden, you think you can swim? Your shoulder is hurt." Caden said, "I'm fine now, my shoulder is not hurting anymore." Maya kept looking at Caden, Caden said, "I am going to change, I will meet you there." Maya said, "OK." Caden kissed Maya then got up and started walking away. Blake, Pacey, and Taylor were swimming. They were waiting for Maya, Quinn, Emily and Caden. Caden came, and got in the water, Caden said, "It's so cold!" Blake said, "Keep swimming, you will get warm." Caden looked around to make sure Maya wasn't there. Caden said, "Guys, do any of you have Tvlenol? I have a headache." Pacey said, "I have some in my bag, I'll go get it now." Caden said, "I don't want Maya to know, you know how she is. She will make me get more rest, and not let me do anything." Blake said, "She's just worried about you. She loves you." Pacey got out of the pond, Caden said, "I love Maya, but I don't want her to be worried about me. I want her to have a good time, Pacey, I'll go with you." Pacey said, "Ok." Caden got out of the pond too. They started walking away. Blake said, "I am going to check on Quinn, and see what's taking her so long." Taylor said, "Ok." Blake was ready to get out of the pond, but Quinn interrupted. Quinn said, "Blake." Blake looked over at Quinn. Blake said, "I thought you weren't coming." Quinn said, "I didn't want to, but Emily and Maya begged me to. I hate cold weather." Blake was smiling. Blake said, "You don't have to swim." Blake got out of the pond; Blake went to Quinn. Quinn said, "I'll go swimming tomorrow." Blake Said, "Ok." Blake kissed Quinn. Maya was looking for Caden. Maya said, "Where is Caden?" Blake said, "With Pacey, they will be back." Maya said, "Is he ok?" Blake said, "He's fine, don't worry. I know you are worried about Caden, but he's fine." Maya said, "Ok." Emily said, "Blake's right." Maya was ready to speak, but Caden interrupted. Caden grabbed Maya, then pulled her to him. Caden whispered to Maya. Maya was looking at Caden Pacey went in the pond. Pacey swam over to Taylor. Maya said, "Caden, are you going to swim?" Caden said, "No, it's too cold, I don't want you to swim either. You'll get sick." Maya said, "I thought you wanted to go swimming." Caden said, "I' d like to swim now, but I don't want you to get a cold." Maya said, "Ok." Caden said, "I know you don't want to swim, you were just going to, for me." Maya was quiet. Caden said, "Am right?" Maya said, "I know you want to have a good time." Caden said, "And spend it with you." Caden kissed Maya. Blake said, "What are we going to do tomorrow?" Quinn said, "We don't know, we will find out tomorrow." Blake said, "OK." Emily said, "I am going to swim." Caden said, "It's too cold." Emily didn't listen to him. Emily went to the pond. Emily gasped. Emily said, "It's so cold!" Caden said, "I told you." Emily got out of the pond. Emily said, "I'm not going swimming tonight." Maya said, "I'm glad that I didn't get in." Caden said, "I will throw you in the pond." Maya said, "You better not," Caden said, "I will." Maya knew that Caden would. Maya tried to get away from him, Caden was ready to grab Maya, but Maya got away from him again. Maya said, "Don't." Caden tried to run to Maya, but Maya ran away. Caden was chasing Maya. Pacey and Taylor got out of the pond. Taylor was shaking. Quinn said, "Cold?" Taylor said, "Very." Pacey held Taylor tight, Pacey was trying to keep her warm. Blake said, "Looks like Caden feels better now." Emily said, "He is fine." 'Taylor said, "He has a headache." Emily said, "We didn't know." Taylor said, "Caden doesn't want Maya to know, He doesn't want her to be worried about him." Quinn said, "But Caden looks like he is fine, he's playing around with her now." Pacey said, "Caden's just doing that because he doesn't want Maya to know that he has a headache. Caden needs to take it easy." Taylor said, "Talk to him Pacey." Pacey said, "I will try, come on." Everyone went to their cents. Maya and Caden were kissing. Pacey said, "Caden, need to talk with you." Caden said, "Ok." Pacey said, "In private." Caden said, "I will be back." Maya said, "Ok." Caden and Pacey were walking away. Maya was looking at Caden. Emily went to Maya. Emily said, "Maya, are you ok?" Maya said, "I am fine." Emily said, "How is Caden?" Maya said, "I just asked him. He said he feels fine." Emily said, "That's good." Maya looked at her.

The girls were asleep, but Emily was cooking breakfast for them. Caden, Blake and Pacey were walking over in the woods. Pacey said, "Caden, you feel any better?" Caden said, "A lot better, I got a text from Trey. He said that him and Ashley got back together again." Pacey said, "Finally!" Blake said, "Yeah, Caden, Is your phone battery still good?" Caden said, "It's 70% now, I turned it off, to save battery." Pacey said, "I should bring my phone, and keep it off." Blake said, "Me too." Caden said, "Blake, you know Parker left this morning." Blake said, "That's good." Caden said, "I was wondering are you and him ok?" Blake said, "I guess so. Parker didn't want to do that to me, that's why he left, but I don't trust him." Caden said, "I know, I bet you feel better now that he moved out." Blake said, "I do." Pacey said, "What about Quinn?" Blake said, "She knew he moved out, but I don't know if she is happy about it. Quinn knows that Parker has a crush on her, but I am afraid that will lose Quinn, what if Parker changes his mind, and moves back, and tries to steal Quinn from me?" Caden said, "Quinn wouldn't do that. She told you that she doesn't want him, she wants you, and she loves you." Blake said, "I know, but what if Parker gets her to change her mind about me? I can't lose her; I love her with all of my heart." Caden said, "Parker won't do that, Parker loves you, like a brother, and Quinn loves him like a brother too, Quinn loves you, I know she wouldn't do that to you, and he told me that he had to leave, it's hard for him because you are his best friend. He can't do that to you, and he doesn't want to be around Quinn. He is trying." Blake interrupted, Blake said, "I know, but am afraid" Caden said, "You are going to be fine, and you won't lose Quinn. I know Parker wouldn't do that to you." Blake said, "I don't trust Parker." Caden and Pacey looked at Blake. Blake said, "Pacey, do you remember Pagie?" Pacey said, "Oh, yeah, I forgot about her." Caden said, "Who is Pagie?" Blake said, "I used to like this girl Pagie, Parker knew, but Parker asked Pagie out anyway, and lied to me, Parker said he didn't know that I liked her." Pacey said, "You were upset about it." Blake said, "I wanted to take Pagie out, but Parker stole her from me, now I am really scared that I will lose Quinn to him." Pacey said, I know but Parker's a changed man now. Parker doesn't want to do that to you again, that's why he decided to move out, he doesn't want to have to see you two." Blake said, "I know." Caden said, "Now that Parker moved out, you don't have to worry about him." Blake said, "I know, but there's one thing I'm worried about." Pacey said, "What?" Blake said, "Text. They will text each other." Pacey said, "If they did start texting again, you could ask Quinn to let you read the texts." Blake said, "No, I don't want her to think I'm trying to be her boss or control her." Caden said, "Does Quinn know about Pagie?" Flake said, "No." Pacey said, "You need to tell her about Pagie." Balce said, "I'm going to today." Caden said, "Good, you both are going to be ok. I know Quinn wouldn't do that to you, she is crazy about you." Blake said, "I'm crazy about her too." Pacey said, on, I bet they are wondering where we are." Blake said, "Ok." They were walking towards the girls, Caden said, "Maya." Maya looked at him, Maya said, "Where were you?" Caden said, "We were walking around!" Maya said, "Oh." Caden kissed her. Pacey sat with Taylor. Blake said, "Is Quinn still asleep?" Emily said, "Blake, Quinn was crying." Blake said, "Why? Is she okay?" Emily said, "She thought." Quinn interrupted, Quinn said, "Blake, don't listen to her." Blake was looking at Quinn. Blake said, "You weren't crying?" Quinn said, "No." Emily said, "I was joking." Blake said, "You scared me." Emily laughed, Emily said, "Sorry." Quinn said, "When I asked her where you went to, Emily was picking on me about you." Blake said, "Oh." Blake pulled Quinn to him, Blake said, "We need to talk." Quinn said, "What about?" Blake said, "About Parker." Quinn said, "I don't want to talk about him again." Blake said, "I know, but need to talk to you about him and Pagie." Quinn said, "Who is Pagie?" Blake said, "I will explain it you." Quinn sighed, and said, "Ok." Blake and Quinn started walking away from their friends. Blake said, "Do you know Paige Brown?" Quinn said, "I think so." Blake explained what happened to her. Quinn said, "Wow, I know." Blake said, "That's why I am afraid." Quinn said, "You need to stop worrying about that, I won't do that to you, I love you, forget him." Blake said, "I am worried, because you and Parker text each other, and." Quinn said, "I will stop texting him." Blake said, "I can't make you do that." Quinn said, "You're not making me." Quinn kissed him. Quinn said, "We don't need to worry about him." Blake looked at her. Quinn said, "I'm hungry, come on." Blake said, "OK." They went back to their friends. Blake sat down. Quinn went to Emily, Caden was looking at Blake. Caden said, "Everything ok?" Blake said, "Everything's great." Caden said, "That's good." Quinn came back and gave Blake a plate of food. Blake said, "Thanks." Quinn was sitting with Blake. Pacey said, "You all know Trey and Ashley are back together again?" Quinn said, "How do you know?" Pacey said, "Caden told us, Trey texted him." Quinn said, "Caden, did you bring your phone?" Caden said, "Yeah I've kept it turned off so I could save battery." Quinn said, "I didn't know that you brought your phone." Maya said, "Caden always take it with him when he goes somewhere." Caden said, "So I can take pictures of you." Maya glanced at him. Caden smiled. Maya said, "You know I hate pictures." Caden said, "I know." Maya said, "What did Trey say about Ashley?" Caden said, "Trey was just excited that we're back together again, that's all." Emily said, "I am so happy that they are together again, Ashley really loves him." Pacey said, "Emily, why don't you get a boyfriend?" Emily said, "I'm not ready for a boyfriend, I want to be single for a while." Pacey said, "You need to forget about Auggie," Emily said, "I'm not worried about him, I like to be alone." Pacey said, Caden said, "Auggie's crazy about you." Emily said, "No, I don't like him." Caden said, "I thought you were crazy about him, because you wouldn't go with anyone else" Emily said, "I'm not." Caden was to speak, but Maya interrupted, Maya said, "Nick really likes you, Em." Emily looked at Maya. Caden said, "My cousin Nick?" Emily said, "How do you know?" Maya said, "Nick kept looking at you, and when you weren't with us,

Nick talked about you a lot. I know he likes you." Emily said, "I didn't know that" Maya said, "I think you would be a cute couple." Emily said, "I'm not ready to date anyone." Maya said, "I think you would like him if you hung out with him, he is really funny." Emily said, "Nah, I want to be alone for a while." Taylor said, "Wait and see." Emily said, "Ok." Emily was quiet. Caden said, "I didn't know that Nick liked Emily." Maya said, "He kept looking at her, and he kept talking to us about Emily." Caden said, "He didn't t say anything to me about Emily." Maya said, "She is our best friend, he wanted to know about her, that's why he asked us about Emily." Caden said, "Why didn't he ask her out?" Maya said, "We don't know." Blake said, "If Nick asks you out, what you will say to him?" Emily said, "I don't know, I don't know him very well." Caden said, "Nick's a good man." Taylor said, "You know him, you've talked to him a lot." Emily said, "But we stopped talking now." Quinn said, "Why?" Emily said, "I guess We don't have time to talk, I was very busy." Maya said, "Or you are trying to avoid him?" Emily said, "No, I'm not trying to avoid him. I just don't have time." Quinn said. "Ok." Emily said, "Let's not talk about that." Maya said, "Why not?" Emily said, "Because I don't want to." Caden looked at Emily. Caden said, "Did something happened to between you two?" Emily said, "No." Caden said, "You acted weird when we were talking about Nick," Emily said, "No I didn't." Maya said, "Yeah you did." Caden said, "I think he has asked you out." Emily said, "He hasn't asked me out." Caden kept looking at Emily. Emily wouldn't look at Caden, and Maya. Caden said, "Ok."

Caden and Pacey were talking about his wedding. Pacey was nervous. Pacey said, "Do you think Taylor won't change her mind about marrying me?" Caden said, "No, she won't, she loves you, I know she wants to marry you." Pacey looked at Taylor. Pacey said, "I really love her, I don't know what I would do without her." Caden said, "I know you love her, next week you both will get married." Pacey said, "I can't wait." Pacey kept looking at Taylor. Caden said, "When we get out of here, we are going to have a party." Pacey said, "Where are we going to have it?" Caden said, "I will ask Blake about that." Pacey said, "Ok.' Caden said, "You will be fine." Pacey said, "I know, I am just afraid that Taylor will change her mind." Caden said, "She won't." Pacey said, "How do you know?" Caden said, "She loves you, she wants to marry you, she's always talking about it." Pacey said, "Good." Pacey looked at Taylor, then Maya. Pacey said, "Is everything okay with you and Maya?" Caden said, "We are ok now, I'm just worried that when we get back, Erin will try to tell Maya stuff, and try to get her to break up with me again." Pacey said, " I think she won't. She learned her lesson," Caden said, "I need to do something to get Erin to let us go." Pacey said, "You are going to talk to her?" Caden said, "No, don't want to go around her alone, it will make Maya think that I want to get with her. I need someone go talk to her for me." Pacey said, "What about your cousin Peyton? Peyton don't like Erin." Caden said, "I don't want her to get in trouble. She almost got in trouble because of Erin before." Pacey said, "What did she do?" Caden said, "Peyton went to Erin's house, and tried to fight her, Erin got scared, and called the police." Pacey said, "When did that happen?" Caden said, "I think it was a month ago." Pacey said, "Why did Peyton want to fight Erin?" Caden said, "Peyton likes Maya, Peyton was hoping we would stay together and get married, and Erin kept telling Maya stuff. Peyton was mad about that, so she went to Erin, and tried to get her to stop trying to do that to us, but Erin wouldn't, so she tried to fight to get her to fight." Pacey said, "I knew Erin was scared of Peyton, at school, she tried to go over to Erin, Peyton just wanted to talk with Erin, but Erin got scared, and left." Caden said, "I don't want Peyton to talk to Erin again, Erin will try to get her in trouble," Pacey said, "I understand, I will try to find someone to talk to Erin for you." Caden said, "Thanks." Pacey said, "No problem." Caden said, "I'm scared I'll lose Maya." Pacey said, "You have to keep Maya away from Erin." Caden said, "I can't, Erin will go to Maya's house, and bother her." Pacey said, '"Why doesn't Maya call the police on her when she does?" Caden said, "I don't know." Blake came over, Blake said, "Hey." Blake sat down with them. Blake said, "What's up?" Caden said, "Nothing much, we were just talking about Erin." Blake said, "Oh, forget her." Caden said, "I am, but I am worried when we get back, Erin will keep trying to get Maya to break up with me again." Blake said, "We won't let that happen again." Caden said, "How? We can't." Blake said, "We will keep Erin away from Maya.' Caden said, "She will go to Maya's house." Blake said, "You need to talk to her mom about that, if Erin goes to her house again, Tell Maya's mother to call the police" Caden said, "Ok. I will talk with Mrs. Post." Blake said, "Mrs. Post loves you," Caden said, "How do you know that Mrs. Post likes me?" Blake said, "When you and Maya broke up, Mrs. Post was upset, she didn't want you two to break up." Caden said, "I didn't know." Blake said, "You need to stop thinking about Erin, and need to stop worrying about Parker and Quinn too." Caden said, "You're still worried about Parker and Quinn?" Blake said, "I'm trying not but I can't." Pacey said, "You know that Quinn won't do anything, Quinn is not like Pagie." Blake said, "I know." Caden said, "Quinn loves you." Blake said, "I love her too, I am scared to lose her to Parker." Caden and Pacey were looking at Quinn, Maya, Emily, and Taylor. They knew Quinn heard Blake. Caden said, "Hey, Girls." Blake turned to the girls. Quinn sighed. Maya went to Caden. Taylor was sitting with Emily. They are quiet. Quinn went to Taylor and Emily. Blake knew that Quinn was mad at Blake. Blake said, "Quinn." Quinn looked at Blake. Blake said, "Are you mad at me?" Quinn said, "No. I'm not, but I'm very tired, you keep thinking that I will get with Parker, I don't want Parker, I told you many times that I love you, with all my heart, not Parker, I love him as a brother." Blake said, "Quinn." Quinn interrupted. Quinn said, "I don't want to talk about that again." Blake was quiet. Quinn sat with Emily and Taylor. Quinn was talking with Taylor and Emily. Caden and Maya were whispering to each other. Pacey said, "Blake, Quinn will talk to you soon." Blake said, "You two should've warned me when the girls came." Pacey said, "We didn't know." Blake was quiet. Blake was looking at Quinn. Pacey said, "You need to stop thinking about Quinn and Parker." Blake said, "I know." Blake looked at Pacey. Blake said, "I'm just scared that Parker will try to steal her from me." Pacey said, "But Parker moved out, you don't have to worry about that." Blake said, "I know, but what if Parker comes back and cried to steal her?" Pacey said, "If Parker does try that, I know Quinn wouldn't, you have to talk to Quinn about that later." Blake said, "Ok." Blake was watching Quinn; Quinn was ignoring him. Maya whispered, "Do you think they will be ok?" Caden was looking at Quinn and Blake. Caden said, "They will be ok, Quinn was upset, but Quinn and Blake will be ok." Maya was looking at them. Caden said, "Maya." Maya looked at him and he kissed her. Maya, Emily, Taylor, and Quinn were talking. Caden and Pacey were making a campfire. Blake kept looking at Quinn. Quinn wouldn't talk to him all night. Blake decided to try to get her to talk with him. Blake went over to Quinn. Blake said, "Quinn, we need to talk." Quinn said, "If it's about Parker, I don't want to talk about him again." Quinn turned away, Blake said, "Quinn." Quinn looked back at Blake again. Blake said, "We need to talk." Quinn said, "I'll be back." Emily said, "Ok." Quinn started walking away from the guys. Blake was following her. Caden and Pacey were watching them, Caden said, "They will work it out." Pacey said, "You're right." Caden was looking at the campfire. Maya went over to Caden. Maya said, "I'm cold." Caden said, "Let me keep you warm." Caden pulled her to him and held her tight. Taylor and Emily walked over to them. Taylor said, "Do you think Quinn and Blake will be ok?" Caden said, "They will be fine, you know how they are, they always argue and then make up." Taylor said, "You are right." Caden said, "Let them talk in private." They were all sitting. Emily said, "Taylor, Pacey, you two are getting married next week, are you guys ready?" Taylor looked at Pacey. Pacey said, "I'm ready, Taylor?" Taylor knew that Pacey was scared that Taylor would change her mind, Taylor decided to joke with Pacey. Taylor said, not ready to get married, I think we should change the plan." Pacey was looking at Taylor. Pacey said, "You don't want to get married next week?" Taylor kept looking at Pacey, Taylor tried not to laugh, but Taylor couldn't hold it in, Taylor started laughing. Pacey said, "What?" Taylor said, "I was joking!" Pacey kept looking at Taylor, Taylor said, "Of course I am ready to get married." Pacey sighed, Pacey pulled Taylor to him, Taylor was still laughing at Pacey. Pacey said, "You scared me." Taylor whispered, "I know, but I won't change my mind, I love you with all my heart." Pacey smiled, Pacey said, love you with all my heart." Emily said, "I am glad that you two are still getting married, I thought Taylor changed her mind," Caden said, "Us too." Taylor was laughing, Taylor said, "I won't." Taylor kissed Pacey. Taylor said, "I love him with all my heart, I won't," Pacey said, "That's good." Pacey kissed her, they heard Quinn and Blake arguing. Pacey looked at Caden. Pacey said, "Do you think we should go and stop them?" Caden said, "I guess so." Caden was ready to get up, but Maya interrupted. Maya said, "Let them be." Caden looked at her. Emily said, "They will be fine." Caden said, "Ok." Caden sat down. They looked at Blake, and Quinn. Caden said, "Looks like Quinn is really mad." Maya said, "I know, let them be, they need to work it out." Caden said. Maya kissed Caden. Pacey said, "I'm glad that Parker's gone." Emily said, "Parker is your best friend, why are you glad that he left?" Pacey said, "If Parker hadn't left, Blake and Quinn would've broken up, because Blake would've done something, and Quinn would have been even more mad." Caden said, "You're right, Pacey." Emily said, "Quinn told me about Pagie, I didn't know about that." Pacey said, "Blake really liked her, Parker knew that, but he asked her out anyway." Emily said, "Why did Parker do that to Blake? They are best friends." Pacey said, "I don't know, but think Parker has changed, Parker left, because of Quinn. He didn't try to steal Quinn from Blake. I told Blake that Parkers changed." Emily was looking at Quinn and Blake. Caden said, "Emily, talked with Nick for a bit today." Emily looked at Caden. Maya said, "Did Nick ask about Emily?" Caden said, "Nick wanted to know how Emily was doing, and if Emily had a boyfriend." Emily said, "Yeah, right, you didn't talk to Nick." Caden said, "He said when we get back, he's going to talk to you." Emily was quiet, Emily wouldn't look at Caden and Maya. Maya knew that Emily really liked Nick, but she didn't want them to know. Maya said, "Em, you like him." Emily said, "As friend." Maya said, "I think you really like him?" Emily wouldn't answer her, Maya said, "Emily, let's talk in private." Emily was ready to speak, but Maya interrupted, Maya got up, and grabbed Emily's elbow. Maya pulled her away from their friends. Maya said, "Did something happened between you and Nick?" Emily said, "No, why are you and Caden." Maya interrupted again, Maya said, "You were acting weird again, I know something happened, you don't want us to know." Emily said, "Nick asked me out." Maya said, "You went out with him?" Emily said, "We went out a few times." Maya kept looking at Emily. Emily said, "I told him am not ready to date anyone." Maya said, "Why?" Emily said, "I'm scared." Maya said, "You think Nick will hurt you like Auggie." Emily said, "'I guess so." Maya said, "Nick would never cheat on with other girls." Emily said, "Maya, I don't want anyone to know." Maya said, "I won't say anything." Emily said, "Auggie did hurt me." Maya said, "I know, Augie cheated on you a lot." Emily said, "And hit me." Maya was looking at Emily. Maya was shocked. Maya said, "What?" Emily said, "That's why I am scared to date anyone. What if I find someone like Auggie? I don't want to get hurt again." Maya said, "I didn't know that. Why didn't you tell me?" Emily said, "I knew you; Quinn, Ashley and Taylor would go after Auggie. I don't want you all to." Maya said, "Ok, but Nick is not like Auggie, Nick would never hurt you, I know him." Emily said, "What if you are wrong?" Maya was looking at Emily again, Maya said, "Why don't you ask Caden about Nick, you can get to know him more." Emily interrupted, Emily said, "No, I don't want to." Maya said, "Come on, you need to stop being scared." Emily said, "I know but." Maya interrupted. Maya said, "Just try and stop, and go out with Nick again, if you are not happy, then you don't have to go again." Emily said, "I really like Nick, but I am scared." Maya said, "I will always be here for you." Emily was looking at Maya. Maya said, "If you still are scared, came to me, we will talk." Emily said, "Let me think." Maya said, "ok." Maya and Emily were walking back to their friends. They were watching Quinn and Blake, Quinn was ready to walk away from Blake, but Blake pulled Quinn to him, and kissed her. Quinn pushed Blake away. Quinn was talking to Blake again. Maya said, "I guess they are still arguing." Caden said, "They will kiss and make up soon." Maya said, "How do you know?" Caden said, "We know how they are, look at them." Maya was looking at them again. Quinn kept talking to Blake, Blake pulled Quinn to him again, Blake said, "Kiss me." Quinn was looking at Blake, then Quinn kissed Blake, Caden said, "I told you so, Maya." Maya was looking at Caden, then Maya went to Caden, and sat down with him. Caden kissed Maya. Caden said, "I love you, Maya."

Maya said, "I love you too." Maya was thinking about Emily and Auggie. Emily looked at Quinn and Blake, then back at her friends. Maya kept looking at Emily. Pacey said, "Em, when we get back. Nick's going to ask you out, you going to go out with him or what?" Emily said, "I really don't know." Taylor said, "Come on, you need to find someone. Forget Auggie." Emily said, "I don't want to talk about Aggie." Taylor said, "Ok." Pacey said, "Nick is a good guy." Emily said, "I know." Blake and Quinn came back. Blake said, "Sorry." Caden said, "It's fine, now is everything okay?" Blake was looking at Quinn. Quinn was quiet. Caden knew that Quinn was still mad at Blake. Blake said, "Quinn?" Quinn said, "We are fine." Caden said, "That's good." Quinn was sitting with Emily and Taylor. Blake was looking at Quinn. Caden said, "Are we going to another place tomorrow?" Blake said, "I guess so, if you guys want to." Maya said, "Why don't we stay here? I like it here." Quinn said, "Me too." Blake said, "Ok, we are going to stay here." Maya said, "Good." Maya was looking around. Emily said, "When you both get married, where are you going to take Taylor, Pacey?" Pacey said, "I can't say." Taylor said, "He won't tell me, He doesn't want me to know," Caden said, "And he doesn't want us to know either. He thinks we will follow them." Blake said, "We won't." Pacey said, "Taylor, I kept forgetting to let you know that Mom wanted to talk with you!" Taylor said, "Why?" Pacey said, "I don't know, I think it's about the wedding. Taylor said, "Oh, ok." Blake was looking at Pacey. Pacey caught him. Blake mouthed to Pacey, "Will Parker be there?" Pacey mouthed, "I think so." Blake was quiet. Quinn was watching Blake. Quinn was thinking about Blake. Blake did not know that Quinn was watching Blake. Quinn said, "Caden, can I borrow your phone?" Caden said, "Sure."

Caden was walking around, and he was looking for his phone. He couldn't find it. Pacey was helping him look. Maya came over, Maya said, "What are you guys doing?" Caden said, "We are looking for my phone." Maya said, "You lost your phone?" Pacey said, "I bet it was because he kept thinking about you and lost it." Maya said, "How did you lose it?" Caden said, "I don't know, Quinn gave it back to me then, I put it in the tent, now it's not there." Maya said, "Did you ask everyone if they have seen it?" Caden said, "I asked them, they haven't seen it." Maya said, "Oh, I wonder how you lost your phone." Caden was looking at Maya, Caden knew that she was panicking. Caden pulled Maya to him, Caden said, "Why are you panicking?" Maya said, "I'm not." Caden interrupted, Caden said, "You are." Maya said, "What if someone went in your tent, and stole it? "Caden said, "No, I don't think so, I lost it, no one stole my phone." Maya said, "Why can't you find it?" Caden said, "I don't know, maybe an animal got it." Maya said, "If an animal got it, then why didn't the animal try to get you?" Caden said, "I don't know, don't worry, everything will be ok." Maya was quiet, Caden kissing her, Caden whispered, "You are so cute when you are all panicking." Maya was looking at Caden. Blake came over, Blake said, "Found your phone, Caden?" Caden said, "No." Blake said, "Oh, I wonder how you lost it." Maya said, "Me too." Pacey said, "Maya's panicking now, she thinks someone went in his tent, and stole it." Blake said, "Maya, there is no one here, you don't need to panic, like Quinn." Maya said, "I didn't know that Quinn was panicking." Blake said, "She's okay now." Maya said, "Good." Caden said, "You two ok now?" Blake said, "We are ok now, I kept talking with her, finally." Caden said, "That's good." Pacey said, "I am going to Taylor." Pacey walked away. Blake said, "I am going to swim, want to join us?" Caden said, "I will be there in a few minutes." Blake said, "Ok." Blake walked away. Caden was looking at Maya. Caden said,

"Go ahead, I will be there." Maya said, "No, I am going to look for your phone." Caden said, "You don't have to." Maya said, "Looks like you don't want me to be with you, you are trying to." Caden interrupted. Caden said, "I do want you to be with me, but I want you to have a good time with your friends, not be looking for my phone and miss out." Maya said, "Let me." Caden looked at her, Caden said, "Come on." They were looking for the phone. They couldn't find it. Caden sighed. Maya said, "I bet you excited that you can't find your phone, so you are going to get new one." Caden said, "No, I don't want to lose my phone, I lost a lot pictures, and I took some pictures of you here." Maya was looking at Caden, Maya said, "What?" Caden said, "You didn't know, but Quinn and Emily knew, we didn't want you to know, if you knew, you would've snuck, and stole my phone, and deleted the pictures of you." Maya said, "You are right, I am glad that you lost the pictures, but am not glad that you lost your phone." Caden said, "I know, but when get a new one, I am going to take pictures of you again." Maya said, "You better not." Caden smiled, Caden pulled her to him, they were kissing. Caden said, "I am glad that you came." Maya said, "Me too." They were ready to kiss again, but Quinn interrupted them. Quinn said, "Maya." They turned to Quinn, Quinn said, "Sorry, I didn't know you guys were busy." Caden said, "It's ok." Quinn said, "I came to see if Maya wanted to swim with us." Caden said, "Maya, go, I will be there in a few minutes." Maya said, "Ok." Maya kissed him. Quinn said, "Did you guys find the phone?" Caden said, "No." Quinn said, "You will find it soon." Caden said, "I think I will find it." Quinn said, "I'll be at the pond, waiting for you, Maya." Maya said, "Ok." Quinn walked away. Maya said, "Are you coming to the pond?" Caden said, "In a few minutes." Maya "I will wait for you." Maya kissed him, then walked away. Caden looked at Maya, then around. Caden was thinking about his phone, he was wondering how he had lost it. He started walking around, Caden decided to give up on looking for his phone, Caden walked to his friends at the pond, Maya said, "You came." Caden said, "I told you I would." Maya said, "I know, but I thought you wouldn't come." Caden said, "Why aren't you swimming with them?" Maya said, "The water is too cold." Caden said, "Oh." Maya turned away, Caden grabbed Maya, Maya gasped. Caden whispered to her, Maya said, "Don't!" Caden said, "We will play around, you will get warm?" Maya said, "No! don't want to swim." Caden said, "Swim with me." Maya said, "No." Caden wouldn't listen to her, Caden pulled her, and threw her in the pond. Maya gasped. Caden jumped in the pond. Maya said, "You are getting paid back!" Caden was laughing. Caden said, "Nah." Caden was picking on Maya. Everyone swam for a while. Someone was watching them. Caden's phone rang, everyone heard it. Caden was looking around. Blake said, "I think it's over there." Blake pointed towards the woods. Caden said, "I am going out there." Blake said, "I'm going with you." Caden said, "Ok." Maya grabbed Caden, Maya said, "Don't go." Caden said, "It's ok, I am going to go get my phone back, I will be back." Caden and Blake got out of the pond. Maya was looking at them. Taylor said, "They are ok, Maya." Maya said, "You are right." Caden and Blake left. Maya said, "I am going to get out, I'm too cold." Quinn said, "Me too. Emily said, "I am going to cook," Caden and Blake was walking over in the woods, they were looking for the phone, but they couldn't find it. Someone ran, Blake saw someone, Blake said, "Hey!" Caden was looking at Blake. Blake said, "Who is there?" No one answered. Blake started walking away, Caden said, "Blake?" Blake said, "I thought I saw someone over there." Caden was looking around. Caden followed him, they couldn't find anyone. Blake said, "I think we better go, make sure everyone is ok." Caden said, "You think someone is here?" Blake said, "I think so." Caden was looking at him. Blake said, "Maybe Frank." Caden said, "So, Frank is here to hurt you and me." Blake said, "You are right, we have to get out of here." Caden said, "Right now?" Blake said, "It's getting dark, we have to wait until morning." Caden said, "Come on, let's make sure everyone is ok." Blake and Caden was walking away, Caden said, "I don't want Maya to know about that, you know her, she always panics." Blake said, "I know, I don't want the girls to know either." Caden was quiet. Maya was quiet. Emily and Quinn were cooking. Taylor and Pacey were talking. Maya kept thinking about Caden and the phone. Quinn looked at her, Quinn knew that Maya was worried about Caden. Quinn said, "Maya, Caden's ok." Maya said, "I know." Emily said, "Maya, we're fine, no one is here." Maya interrupted, Maya said, "I know but I've had a funny feeling ever since we got here, what if Frank followed us." Emily said, "He didn't, we saw him leave." Maya said, "Ok." Maya was quiet. Emily started cooking again, Maya sat down. Emily looked at her, Emily said, "I'm going to go try to talk to Maya, I'll be right back." Quinn said, "Ok." Emily went over Maya, Emily said, "We need to talk, come on." Maya said, "Where are we going?" Emily didn't answer. Emily pulled her along. They went into the woods, so they could talk in private. Emily said, "You need to stop worrying so much, No one's here to hurt us." Maya said, "I know, but what if it's Frank. He followed us?" Emily said, "No, I told you that we saw him leave." Maya said, "I know, but he knows where we are, we always come here." Emily interrupted, Emily said, "I know, but we are at a different place now, he won't know where we are!' Maya said, "I guess you are right." Emily said, "Guess? no, I know I am right, we saw Frank get in the car, and drive away, if he came back, we would've heard him." Maya said, "You're right, let's not talk about it." Emily said, "Forget Frank, let's have a good time, Caden will find his phone, you need to have a good time, and you don't need to panic." Maya said, know." Emily said, "We better go, Quinn and Taylor need us to help cook." Maya said, "Ok, let's go." They started walking out of the woods. Then they heard a noise. They turned and looked around. Emily said, "Is anyone there?" No one answered. They heard another noise, Emily looked around, Emily said, "Come on, Maya." Maya looked around, then They started walking again. They heard a noise again, Emily and Maya gasped, they turned, no one. was there. Maya said, "Come on." Maya knew someone was there. Maya pulled Emily. They started running. Maya and Emily kept looking back, to make sure no one was chasing them. They didn't see Blake and Caden. They ran into Caden and Blake, Maya and Emily gasped. Maya and Emily thought they were someone else, but it was just Caden and Blake. Caden grabbed Maya, Caden said, "What going on?" Emily said, "We think someone's out there." Caden said, "How do you know?" Emily told them what happened. Caden said, "Blake, stay with them." Caden was ready to run, but Maya grabbed him, Maya said, "No, you aren't going." Caden was ready to speak, but Blake interrupted. Blake said, "I'll go, Caden, take them back." Caden said, "Ok." Black ran away. Caden said, "Come on." Maya, Emily, and Caden went back to Quinn, Taylor and Pacey. Quinn was looking for Blake. Quinn said, "Where is Blake?" Emily explained everything co Quinn. Quinn said, "What? why did you let him go out there alone?" Caden said, "Blake will be ok." Quinn said, "Go and get Blake," Pacey said, "Let's wait, if he doesn't come back, we will go after him." Quinn said, "But I don't want him to be alone." Caden said, "Quinn, he will be ok," Qainn sighed. They waited for Blake for a while, Quinn kept walking around, and looking over in the woods. Quinn said, "Caden, you and Pacey, go look for Blake." Caden got up, Caden said, "I will." Blake interrupted. Blake said, "Hey." Everyone looked at him, Quinn over to Blake, and hugged him. Quinn said, "Are you ok? Blake said, "I am fine, I didn't see anyone." Emily said, "We heard noises. Blake said, "We are leaving tomorrow morning." Quinn said, "Why?" Blake said, "I will explain everything to you guys later." Quinn looked at him, Quinn knew something was wrong. Quinn said, "Is everything okay?" Blake said, "Everything is fine, don't worry." Quinn said, "Are you sure? Blake smiled at her, Blake went to Caden, and Pacey. They were whispering to each other. Maya was looking at them. Maya knew something was wrong also. Emily said, "Maya, come on, let's cook." Quinn said, "We are done, you two can eat now." Emily said, "Thanks." Emily pulled Maya away from the boys. Emily didn't want Maya to panic. Emily gave Maya a plate. Maya kept watching the boys. Emily said, "Maya." Maya said. Emily said, "Everything is fine." Maya said, "How do you know? We heard someone out there." Emily interrupted. Emily said, "We are going home tomorrow, we are going to be ok. Caden, Pacey and Blake won't let anything happen to us, the noises we heard, were from animals." Maya was quiet. Emily said, "Eat." Caden was looking at Maya, Caden knew Maya was scared. Caden said, "I have to talk with Maya, she looks scared." Blake said, "Ok." Caden went over to Maya. Caden said, "Are you ok?" Maya said, "I guess so!" Caden said, "You will be ok." Maya said, "I know." Caden said, "I know you are scared, but no one's going to hurt you all. I won't let them." Maya said, "Do you think someone is here?" Caden said, "Blake said he didn't see anyone." Maya said, "Ok." Maya knew that the boys didn't want the girls to get scared, they didn't want the girls to know what's going on. Maya was looking around. Caden pulled her to him and held her tight Caden started whispering to Maya. Quinn was quiet. Quinn was thinking. Taylor said, "Do you think something is wrong?" Quinn said, "I really don't know." Taylor was looking at Blake and Pacey, then Quinn. Taylor said, "I think there's something that they don't want us to know." Quinn said, "That's what I think too." Taylor said, "Do you think it's Frank?" Quinn said, "I don't know, I am scared, if it's Frank, you know what he wants?" Taylor said, "Blake and Caden?" Quinn said, "He wanted them." Maya heard Quinn. Caden didn't hear them. Maya was quiet. Maya was looking at Caden. Caden caught her. Caden smiled. Caden whispered, "Love you." Maya said, "Love too." Maya walked over to Caden and held onto him. Caden held her back, Caden said, "We are going to be ok." Maya didn't answer. Maya was thinking. Caden looked at her, then at Blake and Pacey. Blake was looking at them. Pacey and Blake didn't know that Quinn was by them. Pacey said, "Do you think Frank is here trying to get to you?" Blake said, "And Caden." Pacey said, "What are you going do?" Blake said, "1 don't know, I need to get Quinn out of here." Pacey said, "Why not right now?" Blake said, "It's getting dark, I don't want us to get lost." Pacey said, "You're right." Quinn said, "Blake?" Blake turned to her, Quinn said, "You think Frank is here?" Blake said, "No." Quinn said, "Don't lie, I heard you guys." Blake said, "Quinn." Quinn interrupted, Quinn said, "Don't try to lie to me again." Blake and Pacey looked at each other. Quinn pulled Blake away from Pacey. Pacey was looking at them, Taylor and Emily went over to Pacey. Taylor said, "What is going on?" Pacey looked at them, then at Maya. Pacey said, "I don't want to scare you guys." Taylor said, "Pacey, we need to know." Pacey said, "We think Frank might be here, and trying to hurt Blake and Caden." Taylor said, "Oh, have to get out of here right now." Pacey said, "We can't, because it's getting dark now." Taylor said, "We have to watch Caden and Blake." said, "You all can't, but Blake and Caden will be ok." Emily said, "You're right, but how do you know that Frank is here? Did you guys see him?" Pacey explained to them what Blake and Caden told him. Quinn was looking at Blake. Blake said, "I will be fine." Quinn started to cry. Blake said, "Maybe I'm wrong, and Frank isn't here, but we still have to leave." Quinn whispered, "I want us to leave right now." Blake said, "I'd like to, but we can't, it's getting dark. If we leave now, we will get lost." Quinn whispered, "You're right." Quinn went over to Blake and hugged him. Blake said, "Don't worry, we are going to fine." Quinn said, worried about you." Blake said, "Don't be." Blake kissed Quinn. Quinn whispered, "I'm scared." Blake said, "I know you are scared; I am too." Blake held her tight. Blake said, "We are going to be ok." Quinn was quiet. Blake said, "Come on." They went to their friends. Caden was looking at them, Caden said, "Is everything ok?" Blake looked at Caden. Blake mouthed, "She knows." Caden was quiet. Maya was looking at them. Maya was wondering what Quinn knew about. Maya kept looking at them, Quinn went over to Maya, Quinn said, "Are you ok?" Maya said, "I'm fine." Quinn looked at Taylor and Emily. They smiled. Quinn smiled back. Blake went to Quinn, Blake said, "What did you guys cook?" Blake looked at the food. Blake said, "It looks good." Quinn was quiet. Quinn kept looking at Blake. Emily gave Blake a plate. Blake said, "Thanks." Blake started eating. Emily said, "So, what are we doing tonight?" Pacey said, "Packing our stuff to get ready for tomorrow." Taylor said. "We can pack our stuff tomorrow." Pacey said, "I know, but we are leaving tomorrow morning." Maya looked at them. Maya said, "I want to leave right now." Blake said, "Me too, but it's too dark." Maya sighed. Caden said, "Maya, we are going to be fine." Maya said, "I know there's something you guys don't want us to know." Caden was quiet. Maya said, "You know I hate secrets." Caden said, "I know." Maya said, "What do you guys do not want me to know about?" Caden looked at Blake. Blake was quiet. Maya said, "Is it Frank?" Caden looked at her. Maya said, "I heard Taylor, Emily and Pacey." Caden said, "What did they say?" Maya explained what she heard to Caden. Caden looked at Taylor, Pacey, and Emily. Pacey said, "Sorry, I didn't know she was listening." Caden didn't say anything. He was thinking. Maya said, "We have to get out of here right now." Caden said, "If we leave now, we will get lost, because it's getting dark, I think we better wait till in the morning." Maya said, "If we are waiting." Caden interrupted. Caden said, "We are going to be fine. Don't worry, Frank won't get to us, because he is alone." Maya was quiet. Caden pulled her to him. Caden said, "We are going to be fine." Maya whispered, "Ok."

Quinn, Taylor, and Pacey were walking in the woods. They were on their way to the pond. Taylor and Pacey held onto each other; Quinn was quiet. Quinn was thinking about Blake. Taylor was looking at Quinn. Taylor knew Quinn was worried about Blake. Taylor whispered, "Pacey, Quinn's worried about Blake." Pacey looked at Quinn. Pacey said, "Go and talk to her." Taylor looked at Quinn again, then walked over to her. Taylor said, "Quinn, are you ok?" Quinn said, "I guess so." Taylor said, "Blake's going to be ok." Quinn said, "What if Frank gets Blake?" Taylor said, "No, Blake's going to be fine, Frank won't get Blake, we will get out of here in the morning before Frank can get around Blake." Quinn said, "And go to the police." Taylor said, "Yeah, Caden, and Blake need go to the police." Pacey said, "Quinn, everything will be fine, you will see." Quinn said, "Why did Blake never say anything about Frank?" Pacey said, "Blake didn't want you to worry about him." Quinn said, "I am worried about him right now." Taylor said, "We know, but Blake will be ok." Quinn said, "You are right." Taylor said, "Come on, let's get to the pond. They are waiting for us." Quinn said, "Let's go."

They were walking to the pond. Pacey said, "I will be back." Pacey walked away. Taylor said, "I can't wait to get out of here." Quinn said, "Me too, I want to go home." Taylor said, "When we get back, do you think Ryan will try to bother you?" Quinn said, "I don't know, but I think

Ryan has a new girlfriend." Taylor said, "Who?" Quinn said, "I don't know." Taylor said, "How do you know that Ryan got a new girlfriend?" Quinn said, "Mom saw them, at Walmart." Taylor said, "He got a girlfriend. I'm glad that Parkers moved out, and Ryan got a new girlfriend. Now they'll leave you alone." Quinn said, "Parker hasn't been bothering me." Taylor said, "But we noticed that Parker kept hanging around you, and he flirted with you." Quinn said, "He did not flirt with me." Taylor said, "Parker did, Pacey?" Pacey was looking at them. Pacey said, "What?" Taylor said, "Didn't Parker flirt with Quinn when Parker was with us?" Pacey said, "Parker did, Parker's in love with you, Quinn." Quinn was quiet. Taylor said, "Blake was upset." Quinn said, "Why didn't Blake ever say anything to me about it?" Taylor said, "We don't know," Pacey said, "Blake talked to Parkey about that." Quinn said, "When?" Pacey said, "A month ago. Parker said that he wasn't flirting with you, but we know he was." Quinn said, "Let's not talk about Parker." Pacey said, "Who do you want Blake or Parker?" Quinn said, "Blake. I love Blake, not Parker, you all know that." Pacey said, "I know, but why did you let him flirt with you." Quinn said, "I didn't, I thought he just liked picking on me, that's all, I love him as a brother, but I love Blake with all my heart." Pacey said, "I'm glad that you want Blake, not Parker. Blake was worried about you and Parker. We don't want to see Blake get hurt again." Quinn said, "He won't get hurt again, I'm not going to hurt him, and he doesn't need to worry about that. I would never date Parker. Parker is not my type." Pacey said, "Oh, Parker stole Pagie from Blake, I don't blame him for worrying about that." Quinn was quiet. Quinn was walking around. They did not know someone was there, they were wearing black clothes, and masks. Taylor said, "Forget Parker, you…" Someone interrupted Taylor. They screamed and ran over to Pacey. Pacey turned, and someone jumped to him. They went to the ground, they were fighting. Taylor said, "Pacey!" Taylor was ready to get in between them, but Quinn stopped Taylor. Quinn said, "Don't." Taylor kept screaming, "Pacey!" That man was beating him, Pacey passed out. Taylor said, "Pacey!" again. Quinn pulled Taylor away, they started running. Someone was chasing them. Quinn and Taylor kept screaming. Someone grabbed Taylor and pulled her away from Quinn. Quinn said, "Taylor!" They were trying to stab "Taylor's stomach with a knife, but he couldn't. Taylor kept fighting him. Taylor said, "Quinn, get help!" but Quinn wouldn't leave her, Quinn jumped the guy in the mask. Quinn wasn't going to let him hurt Taylor, but then he hit Quinn, Quinn went to the ground, Quinn groaned. He turned to Taylor, Taylor looked at Quinn, then the guy in the mask. And tried to get away, but he grabbed Taylor, and stabbed her arm. Taylor screamed, he hit Taylor, Taylor went to the ground. Taylor was unconscious. Quinn said, "Taylor!" The man turned to Quinn. Quinn looked at Taylor, then at the guy. He was ready to grab Quinn, but Quinn got away, and started running. He was chasing her. Quinn kept running, and looking back, to make sure he wasn't chasing her. He wasn't there. Quinn stopped running. She was panting. Quinn was looking around. She was getting ready to start running again, Quinn turned, And gasped. He was there, he was ready to stab her, but Quinn pushed him. Quinn was about to tun away, but he grabbed her. They were fighting. Quinn went to the ground; Quinn was looking at him. He was ready to stab her, but Taylor hit his back with tree stick. He went to the ground. Taylor hit someone's back again. Taylor dropped tree stick to the ground, then went to Quinn, Taylor helped her up, but the man grabbed Quinn's ankle. Quinn screamed. He pulled Quinn back to the ground, then stabbed Quinn's leg. Quinn screamed. Taylor kicked him in the face, then Taylor pulled Quinn away from him, Taylor and Quinn started running. The guy that was attacking them groaned. He was angry that he hit the ground. He got up. And started running. He was looking for Quinn and Taylor, but he couldn't find them. He ran away, Quinn and Taylor were hiding behind a tree. They were watching him. Quinn groaned; Quinn looked at her leg. Taylor was crying. Taylor said, "Why does Frank want to hurt us? We haven't done anything to him." Quinn said, "Frank wants to get pay back on Blake and Caden," Taylor said, "We have to get Pacey first, then we are going to Blake and Caden, so we can warn them." Quinn said, "You're right." Quinn was looking around. Taylor said, "He left?" Quinn said, "I think so." Quinn looked at Taylor. Quinn said, "Ready?" Taylor said, "Let's go." They got up. They were ready to start running again, but the guy grabbed Quinn. Taylor and Quinn screamed.

Caden was asleep. He had to get some sleep because he was going to be on watch, to make sure no one came around. Maya was sitting and looking at Caden. Pacey was talking with Taylor and Quinn. They were walking over in the woods because they had to get some water. Blake was packing his stuff. Emily came over, Emily saw that Maya kept looking at Caden. Emily walked over to Mava, Emily said, "Are you ok?" Maya said, "I don't know." Emily said, "Worrying about Caden?" Maya was quiet. Maya looked at Emily, then back at Caden. Maya said, "I am scared." Emily said, "Don't be. He will ok." Maya said, "When we get back, I am going to make him." Taylor and Quinn screamed and interrupted them, Emily and Maya gasped. They looked over to the woods. Caden woke up. Blake came over to them. Blake said, "That's Quinn and Taylor." Caden went over to them. Caden said, "What happened?" Blake said, 'I don't know, I'm going out there. Stay with the girls." Blake ran away. Caden looked at Maya. Maya kept looking over to the woods. Caden pulled Maya to him. Caden said, "They are ok." Caden held her tight. Blake was running and said, "Quinn! Where are you?" Blake kept running and looking for Quinn and Taylor. When he ran into Pacey. Blake said, "Pacey?" Pacey said, "Where is Taylor?" Blake said, "I don't know, I thought you were with them." Pacey said, "Taylor!" Taylor screamed, "Pacey!" Blake said, "That way!" Pacey and Blake started running and saw what happened. Blake ran to them, Blake pushed the guy away from Quinn, and Taylor. The man went to the ground, then turned to Blake and got up, and was getting to run away; but Blake grabbed him, Blake pulled him, and they started fighting. Pacey said, "Taylor, Quinn, get out of here." But Quinn wouldn't. Quinn said, "Blake!" The guy pushed Blake, Blake went to the ground, and the man in the mask ran away. Blake got up, Blake was going to go after him, but Pacey said, "Blake! Quinn needs you." Blake looked at Quinn. And then ran over to her. Blake said, "Are you ok?" Quinn was sobbing. Blake said, "Quinn?" Quinn said, "I'm ok." Blake kept looking at Quinn. Blake saw her leg bleeding. Blake said, "Quinn, your leg is bleeding." Quinn looked at her leg. Blake picked her up, Quinn said, "Blake, put me down, I'm fine." Blake wouldn't listen to her, Blake was carrying her, and walking away. Pacey tore his shirt, Taylor looked at Pacey, Taylor said, "Pacey?" Pacey said, "I'm going to tie your arm." Pacey tied it around Taylor's arm. Pacey looked at Taylor. Pacey said, "Are you sure you're, ok?" Taylor said, "I am fine. I don't understand why Frank wants to hurt us." Pacey said, "Me either, come on, let's go." Taylor and Pacey started walking, but Taylor stopped him, Taylor said, "Are you ok? Did he hurt you?" Pacey said, "I'm fine." Pacey pulled her. They were walking to their friends. Maya and Emily were talking with Quinn. Blake was cleaning Quinn's leg. Emily said, "Quinn, are you ok?" Quinn said, "I am fine." Pacey and Taylor came back. Maya said, "Taylor, your arm." Taylor said, "I am ok, Frank stabbed me." Maya said, "Frank shouldn't be trying to hurt you all." Quinn said, "I know." Maya said, "We have to get out of here right now." Caden said, "We can't." Maya said, "He hurt them, Caden." Caden said, "I know but if we leave right now, we will get lost, we have to wait till in the morning." Maya said, "What if he comes here and try to hurt us again." Caden said, "He won't, because he is alone." Maya sighed. Caden said, "We are going to be fine." Maya was quiet. Caden pulled her to him. Caden said, "We will be ok." Maya didn't say anything, Caden knew that Maya was scared. Blake said, "Caden, I need you to get some rest, tonight, because you have to be on watch." Caden said, "Ok." Caden looked at Pacey and Taylor. Caden said, "You two, ok?" Taylor said, "We are ok." Caden said, "Good, I better go to sleep." Caden walked away. Maya kept looking at Caden. Blake said, "Maya, Caden's right, if we leave now, we will get lost." Maya said, "I know, I'm scared that he will hurt Caden." Blake said, "He won't, he is alone." Maya said, "Then why did Frank hurt Quinn, Taylor and Pacey? He is not scared, if he is alone, he will come to us, he is not afraid of us." Blake said, "Because Quinn and Taylor are girls, Pacey was alone, that's why he went to them, when Pacey and I went to help them, Frank ran away, because he got scared." Pacey said, "He's right." Maya was quiet. Blake looked at Quinn. Blake said, "Are you sure you're, ok?" Quinn said, "I'm fine." Blake kept looking at Quinn. Quinn said, "Really, I am fine." Blake said, "Ok, Emily, get me a white bandage." Emily said, "Ok." Emily ran away. Maya helped Pacey clean Taylor's arm. Maya kept thinking about Caden. Taylor was looking at Maya, Taylor knew Maya was worried about Caden. Taylor whispered, "Caden will be ok." Maya looked at Taylor. Maya whispered, "I know, you're right." Maya wouldn't look at Taylor, Taylor whispered, "We will get out of here tomorrow, Frank will not hurt Caden." Maya looked at her, Maya whispered, "You think we can get out of here before Frank gets to Caden?" Taylor whispered,

"Everything will be ok. Caden will be ok, I don't think Frank will come around Caden."

Emily came over, Emily gave Blake a white bandage, then Emily walked over to Pacey. Emily gave Pacey some white bandages too. Emily went back to Blake and helped Blake. Blake said, "Thanks, Emily." Emily looked at Blake, then at Quinn. Emily said, "You are welcome." Blake got up. Blake said, "You all need to get some rest, so you'll be ready in the morning." Quinn got up. Quinn groaned. Blake grabbed her, Blake said, "Are you ok?' Quinn said, "I am fine." Blake said, "Are you sure?" Quinn said, "Stop asking me if I am ok all the time." Blake said, "I can't." Quinn interrupted. Quinn said, "Blake, I'm fine." Blake looked at Quinn. Quinn kissed Blake, and said, "I'm going to sleep." Blake said, "Do you need me to." Quinn interrupted. Quinn said, "I will be fine, Emily or Maya will help me." Blake said, "If you need anything, just let me know." Quinn said, "I will." Pacey said, "I think Taylor and Quinn need to sleep with Maya and Emily in their tent." Blake said, "Yeah." Quinn said, "Ok." Blake said, "I'll help you, Quinn." They walked over to at Caden. Maya said, "I don't want you to go out there." Caden said, "He said if I go out there, he will let you all go. I don't want him to hurt you guys. I am going out there." Maya said, "I won't let you go!" Caden said, "You can't." Maya interrupted. Maya said, "No!" Caden pulled her to him. Caden said, "Maya, I will be ok, I don't want him to come after you" Caden kissed her, Caden was ready to walk away, but Maya wouldn't let him go. Caden sighed. Caden said, "Pacey." Pacey went over to them, Caden said, "Don't let Maya try to come out there to me when I go. You stay with her." Pacey said, "I won't let her." Caden kissed her again, then Caden looked at Blake, Blake said, "Ready?" Caden said, "Let's go." Blake and Caden walked away. Taylor and Emily held onto Quinn. They wouldn't let her go after Blake. Pacey held Maya, too so she couldn't go to Caden. Blake and Caden went into the woods. Blake said, "Frank, we are here, come talk to us." The guy came to them, with a mask on. Blake said, "Take the mask off. We know who you are." The masked guy said, "You think you guys know me, but you are wrong." Blake said, "Frank, take it off. You don't need to hurt us. We were there for AJ." He said, "No, you weren't," Blake said, "We were there, but he wouldn't let us do anything." He said, "You guys don't care!" He grabbed a tree stick and ran to them and hit Caden's face. Caden went to the ground, and he was knocked out. Blake went to the guy. They started fighting. Blake tried to beat him, but Blake couldn't.

Caden woke up. Caden, Quinn, and Taylor tent. Maya looked at Quinn, Taylor, Blake, and Pacey, then at Caden. Emily was looking at Maya, Emily said, "Maya, everything will be ok." Maya was quiet. Emily said, "Come on, let's go to our tent." Emily pulled Maya to the tent. Caden looked at Maya. Caden was pretending to be asleep, but Caden watched Maya, until she got in the tent, Caden thought about Maya, for a while, then fell asleep. Blake came over. Blake looked at Caden, then around. Blake was sitting on the ground, and He was looking at the campfire, He was thinking about what to do. Then he heard a man screaming. "Blake! Caden!" Blake got up, Blake said, "Frank, come here!" Caden went to Blake. They were looking around, to try to find him. Maya, Emily, Pacey, Taylor, and Quinn came out of their tent. Caden said, "Where are you?" The guy said, "Caden, Blake, I want you two to come here and talk to me." Caden said, "Why don't you come here?" He said, "No, I don't want to, I want you two to come here. If you come out here, I will let everyone go." Caden looked at Blake. Blake sighed. Blake looked at Caden, then at Quinn. Quinn looked at him, Quinn knew that

Blake was going to go out there. Quinn said, "No." Blake said, "We will be back." Quinn said, "He will hurt you." Blake pulled her to him. Maya kept ahold of Caden. Caden looked at Maya. Caden said, "Maya, we are going to be ok, I will be back." Maya was crying. Maya kept looking and groaned. Caden saw them. And went over to them, Caden helped Blake beat him, he went to the ground. Blake kicked his face, he was unconscious. Blake was panting. Blake looked at Caden. Blake went to the guy; he pulled off his mask. It was A.J. Caden said, "A.J.?" Blake looked at Caden. Blake said, "I'm going to find something to tie him up, so he can't try to hurt us again." Caden said, "I will stay here, and watch him." Blake said, "I'll be quick." Blake ran away. Caden was looking at A.J. Caden said, "Why would you do this to us? We were best friends."

Maya was crying. Quinn was thinking about Blake. Emily and Taylor were sitting with them. Pacey was walking around. Blake came back, Blake said, "Pacey." Everyone turned to him, Quinn went to Blake, and hugged him, Maya got up, Maya said "Where is Caden? Blake said, "He's ok, Pacey. Do you have any that I can tie A.J. up with?" Pacey said, "A.J.?" Blake said, "It's not Frank, it's AJ." Everyone was shocked. Maya said, "Why would AJ do this? We were his best friends." Blake said, "I know." Pacey said, "I am going to get rope." Blake and Pacey were walking away. Maya was looking at the girls. Maya said, "They got AJ. We are going to be ok." Quinn said, "Yeah" Quinn sat down, Quinn said, "Why would AJ want to hurt us?" Blake came over, Blake said, "Be right back." Blake ran away with the rope. Pacey walked over and stood by them. Pacey said, "They are going to bring him here." Quinn was looking at the girls.

Caden was looking around, Caden didn't know that woke up, A.J. kept looking at Caden, Caden turned away, A.J. got up. A.J. hit Caden's shoulder with the tree stick. Caden went to the ground. A.J. kept hitting Caden's shoulder with the tree stick. Caden groaned, Caden tried to fight with him, but he couldn't. Blake jumped A.J., They went to the ground. They were fighting. Caden looked at Blake, and Caden got up. He was getting ready to go to them, But A.J. pushed Blake away from him, then A.J. got up, and ran away. Blake started chasing him. Caden groaned, because his shoulder was in pain, Caden was going to go after them, but Blake came back, Blake said, "He got away!" Caden sighed. Blake was panting and looking at Caden. Blake said, "Are you ok?" Caden said, "I'm fine, it's my fault he got away." Blake said, "No, it's not your fault. Let's go." Caden and Blake started walking away. They were on their way to their friends. Caden said, "I don't want Maya to know what happened." Blake said, "Ok, but Maya will notice that you are in pain." Caden said, "I will try to act like I'm fine." Blake said, "Try your best." They went to their friends. The girls and Pacey looked at them. Pacey said, "Where is A.J.?" Blake said, "He got away." Pacey said, "What happened?" Blake said, "We will talk about it in the morning. Have to get some sleep. So we'll be ready for tomorrow." Maya said, "Caden, are you okay?" Caden said, "I'm fine, go to sleep, I will stay here and be on watch." Maya kept looking at Caden. Taylor, Emily and Pacey started walking away from them. Pacey said, "Taylor, we shouldn't have come here." Taylor said, "We are going to be fine; we will go home tomorrow." Pacey was quiet. Quinn and Blake came over. Pacey Said, "How did A.J. get away?" Blake explained to them what happened. Pacey said, "Oh, Caden's ok?" Blake said, "I think so, but he is in pain. He doesn't want Maya to know." Taylor said, "Where is Maya?" Blake said, "Maya will be here in a few minutes, she wanted to talk to Caden." Taylor said, "Oh, I don't think she she'll leave, she is probably going to try to stay with Caden, and make sure he is ok." Blake said, "That's what I think." Quinn said, "We have to get some rest, and get ready for tomorrow." Blake said, "If A.J. comes around you all scream." Quinn said, "We will." Blake said, "Let's go to sleep." Quinn kissed Blake, then went into the tent with Emily. Taylor and Pacey were whispering to each other, then Taylor went into the tent. Pacey said, "We are going to sleep here, and make sure that A.J. doesn't come around." Blake said, "I will be back, I'm going to get a blanket and pillow." Pacey said, "Ok." Blake ran away. Quinn was sitting and talking with Emily and Taylor. Quinn said, "Do you think we will get out of here?" Taylor said, "We will, don't worry, A.J. won't get to us." Quinn was quiet. Emily said, "We are going to be fine." Quinn said, "I'm worried about Blake, He's the one A.J. is after, I don't know why he wants Blake. Blake hasn't done anything to him." Emily said, "I know, I think Frank told him about Blake and Caden." Quinn said, "That's what think, we need to do something to Frank." Taylor said, "Don't, Blake doesn't want you to do that." Quinn said, "Frank needs to leave them alone." Emily said, "I know, let the police take care of that." Quinn said, "They will? I don't think so." Taylor said, "You can't go around him, and try to talk to him, he will try to hurt you." Quinn said, "He needs to leave Blake alone." Emily said, "I know, let the police deal with it." Quinn sighed. Emily said, "Blake's going to be ok." Quinn looked at them. Taylor said, "She's right." Quinn whispered, "Ok." They hugged her, Taylor said, "Quinn, Blake's a strong man, you know that."

Caden and Maya were talking. Caden held Maya. They were sitting on the ground. Maya wouldn't go back to the tent, with Quinn, Emily, and Taylor. She was scared that A.J. would come back and try to hurt him. Caden said, "I got an idea, why don't you go to Quinn, Emily, and Taylor, I will sleep outside, you sleep with them in the tent." Maya looked at Caden. Caden said, "I know you don't want me to be alone, you are afraid that A.J. will hurt me." Maya said, "You are right." Caden said, "Don't be, I am going to be ok, I'm worried about you, I don't want A.J. to hurt you." Maya said, "I will be fine." Caden said, "I will sleep there, you can sleep with them." Maya said, "Ok." Caden got up, Caden helped Maya up, then they went to Maya's tent. Caden said, "I will sleep here, you sleep with them, so you know I am ok, and I can know you are ok too." Maya said, "Ok." Caden kissed her, Maya went into the tent. Blake was lying on the ground. Blake said, "You going to sleep here too?" Caden put a blanket and pillow on the ground, Caden said, "To make sure Maya's ok." Blake said, "And Maya's worried about you." Caden said, "I know, she doesn't need worry about me, but I am worried about her too." Blake said, "Everything will be ok, we will leave here tomorrow, before A.J. gets to us." Caden was quiet. Pacey was sitting, and watching around, to make sure A.J. doesn't come back, Pacey said, "I don't understand why A.J, wants to hurt us, I thought he was our friend." Caden said, "Frank told him lies about us." Pacey said, "We have to try to talk to him." Caden said, "I don't want to try to talk to him when the girls are with us, I know A.J. won't talk to us. He will just try to hurt us, I think we better go to the police, and let them take care of that." Pacey said, "You're right." Blake said, "I better go to sleep, wake me up in four hours, Caden." Caden said, "I will." Blake went to sleep, Pacey said, "Caden, go to sleep, I will wake you up in two hours. Caden said, "Ok." Maya overheard them. Quinn said, "Maya, go to sleep." Maya said, "I can't sleep." Quinn said, "Try." Maya said, "Ok." Maya was lying on the ground, Maya was thinking. Quinn said, "Maya, we are going to be ok." Maya didn't say anything. Emily said, "Quinn's right." Maya said, "I know, but I am worried about Caden." Quinn said, "I'm worried about Blake too." Emily said, "Go to sleep, we have to wake up in the morning." Quinn said, "Ok, Maya?" Maya looked at her, Quinn said, "We are going to be ok." Maya whispered, "Yeah." The girls went to sleep, until Morning, Emily woke up, and looked over at Taylor, and Maya. Emily got out of the tent and went to Blake and Quinn. Quinn and Blake were packing stuff. Emily said, "Quinn, Blake." They turned to her. Emily said, "You guys' are ready to leave?" Quinn was ready to speak, but Caden and Pacey interrupted. They said, "Hey." Blake said, "You two better get ready now." Caden said, "I'm going to wake the girls up." Blake said, "Ok." Caden went to the girls, Caden woke Maya up. Maya yawned and looked at him. Caden said, "We are ready to pack our stuff, then leave." Maya got up. Maya said, "I need to go in the woods," Caden said, "Why?" Maya said, "I really need to go to the restroom." Caden said, "Oh, I am going with you, but not with you, you know what I mean?" Maya said, "I know, let me ask Taylor if she needs to go too." Caden said, "Ok." Caden got out of the tent. Maya got out of the tent, Maya said, "She doesn't need to go." Caden said, "Ok, let's go." They were ready to go over in the woods, but Emily interrupted, Emily said, "Where are you guys going?" Maya said, "I really need to go to the restroom." Emily said, "Oh, I am going with you, I need to go too." Emily went with them; they were walking away. Taylor came out of the tent. They looked at Caden, Maya and Emily, then they went to Blake and Pacey. Blake said, "Where is Caden?" said, "They went in the woods, because Maya needed to go to the bathroom." Blake said, "Oh, hope they don't go far." Caden was waiting for Emily and Maya. Caden said, "Maya?" Maya said, "We are done." Caden said, "Come on." Maya and Emily were getting ready to go to Caden, but A J. jumped him, Caden went to the ground, Caden was ready to turn, but A.J. hit Caden's shoulder with a tree stick four times, then kicked Caden's face. Maya said, "Caden!" AJ. looked at Maya and Emily. Emily knew that A.J. was going to hurt them. Emily grabbed Maya, then Emily pulled her away from there. They started running. A.J. was chasing them. Maya fell, Emily was going to go to help her ger up, but A.J. grabbed Emily, Maya said, "Let her go!" A.J. pushed Emily. Emily went to the ground and hit her ankle on a rack. Emily groaned and touched ankle. Maya looked at her, then at A.J., A.J. went over to Maya, She tried to get away from him, but A.J. grabbed her, and pulled her up. Caden came running to them, Caden said, "Let her go!" A.J. made Maya turn to Caden A.J.'s arm was around Maya's neck. AJ. was holding a knife. Caden said, "Don't hurt her, Maya hasn't done anything to you." A.J.'s said, "Frank told me Maya wasn't worried about me, she was worried about you when it happened to me. I love her!" Caden said, "She was worried about you too." said, "No, she wasn't" Maya said, "A.J., I was worried about you, and Caden too. Frank lied to you." AJ. said, "Don't talk! Maya!" Maya looked at Caden, Caden said, 'You can have me, let her go." Blake came co them. Blake said, "A.J., Don't do that." A.J. said, "Stay away, Blake." Blake looked at Maya, then at A.J. Caden kept trying to talk to A.J., Caden tried get closer to them, A.J. said, "Stay there!" Blake grabbed Caden. Blake said, "A.J., Let her go, we can talk." A.J. said, "I don't want to talk to you all! I want you all to get paid back!" A.J. stabbed Maya's stomach with the knife twice. Maya screamed, Caden said, "No!" A.J. pushed Maya away, then ran away. Maya hit the ground, Caden went to Maya, Caden said, "Are you ok?" Maya looked at her stomach, Caden looked at her stomach too, Caden said, "I'm going to go get him!" Caden was getting ready to chase him, but Maya grabbed Caden, Maya said, "Don't." Emily crawled to Maya, Emily said, "Maya?" Blake came. Caden said, "I have to get A.J." Blake said, "Caden, stay with her, I will go after him, take her to Pacey." Blake ran away. Caden picked her up, Caden started carrying her to Pacey, Taylor, and Quinn, Emily sat down, her ankle was hurting. Quinn looked at Maya. Taylor said, "Maya?" Caden said, "Pacey." Pacey ran to Maya. Caden put her on the ground. Pacey was looking at her stomach. Pacey said, "Taylor, get a bandage and some tape." Taylor ran away. Caden said, "Pacey, you think Maya will be, ok?" Pacey said, "I think so." Caden looked at Maya, Quinn said, "Where is Blake?" Emily said, "He went after A.J." Quinn looked at Emily. Emily knew that she was scared that A.J. would hurt him- Quinn said, "Why did you all let him go after A.J.? He will hurt Blake." Emily said, "Blake's going to be ok," Caden said, "Blake will be back." Quinn was quiet. Caden kept looking at Maya. Taylor came back, and gave Pacey the bandage, and tape. Quinn went over to Maya; Quinn was talking to Maya. Taylor said, "Maya's, ok?" Pacey said, "She needs to go to the hospital." Caden said, "I am going take her there right now." Pacey said, "We're going with you." Caden said, "We need to leave right now," Quinn said, "What about Blake?" Caden said, "Quinn, stay with Maya, I'm going to get Blake, then we can leave." Quinn said, "Ok." Caden was about to walk away, but Maya grabbed Caden's shirt. Maya said, "Blake will be here soon, I'm ok." Caden said, "You need to see the doctor." Maya said, "I know, but I am fine." Caden said, "I know you are ok, but you really need to see the doctor." Pacey said, "Caden's right." Blake came back, Quinn ran to him, and hugged him. Quinn said, "Blake, are you ok?" Blake said, "I am fine. I couldn't find him!" Everyone looked at him. Blake said, "A.J. got away." Pacey sighed. Caden said, "We have to go now. She needs to go to the doctor right now." Blake said, "We have to leave our stuff here, we are going to leave right now." Caden said, "Let's go." Emily got up, Emily groaned, Taylor said, "Emily?" Emily said, "I'm fine, it's my ankle." Pacey said, "Emily, do you think you can walk?" Emily said, "When I try to walk, it hurts, but we have to leave." Taylor went to her, helped her. Emily said, "Thanks." Caden got Maya up and started carrying her. They were walking. Maya said, "You can't carry me all day." Caden said, "I can." Maya said, "What about your shoulder, I know your shoulder is hurting, you can't." Caden interrupted, Caden said, "Don't worry, I am fine, Maya" Maya was looking at him. Maya whispered, "Ok." A.J. screamed, "Blake, Caden!" Everyone was looking around, they couldn't see him, A.J. said, "If you two leave, I am going to go after Quinn and Maya!" Caden looked at Blake, then at Maya. Maya "Don't." Blake said, "Caden, go ahead, I will try to talk to him" Caden said, "Blake, you know what A.J. will do." Blake said, "I know, but Maya needs go to the hospital. Maya needs you." Caden looked at Quinn. Blake said, "Pacey, take care of Quinn for me." Pacey said, "We will." Quinn said, "Blake." Blake looked at her, Quinn said, "You don't have stay around A.J." Blake said, "I have to, if I don't A.J. will go after you." Quinn said, "Let the police take care of A.J., not you." Blake kissed her, Blake said, "If I don't go to him, he will come after us, he will hurt you again, I can't let A.J. hurt you again." Quinn said, "Blake." Blake interrupted, Blake said, "Pacey, when you guys get there, get the police to come here," Pacey said, "I will." Quinn said, "Blake, don't." Blake didn't listen to her. Blake said, "Quinn, I love you, with all of my heart." Quinn was crying Quinn said, "I love you with all my heart too." Blake kissed her, then walked away, Quinn said, "Blake!" Quinn was ready to go to him, but Taylor and Emily grabbed her. Emily said, "Blake will be ok, come on." They pulled her away from there. They were walking away. Blake went to A.J. Blake said, "What do you want?" A.J. said, "Where is Caden?" Blake said, "Caden couldn't come with me, he had to take Maya to the hospital." A.J. said, "I warned you two that if you both didn't come, I would go after them." Blake said, "I know, but let him go, Maya needs him." A.J. said, "I'll go after him after I get you." Blake said, "You don't need to try to hurt us." A.J. said, "I want you all to pay back, because Frank told me that you guys didn't try to help me when those four men beat me." Blake said, "It's not true, Frank lied, we were there and helped you." A.J. ran to Blake, they went to the ground, and started fighting. Pacey said, "I can't remember where to go." Pacey was looking around. Caden said, "I think it's that way." Pacey looked at him. Emily said, "I think I heard a car." Caden said, "Where?" Emily pointed over in the wood. Caden said, "Let's go over there, we can try to get some help." Pacey said, "Maya?" Maya looked at Pacey. Pacey said, "Are you ok?" Maya said, "I'm ok." Pacey knew that Maya was lying, Maya's Face was pale, and she was falling asleep. Caden said, "Maya, don't try to lie." Maya said, "I'm not lying, I'm just tired!" Caden looked at Pacey. Caden said, "Is she okay?" Pacey said, "She's lost a lot of blood, that's why she feels so tired, she really needs to go to the hospital, come on." Caden said, "We have to hurry up." Pacey said, "I know." They started walking again. Maya whisper, "Caden?" Caden looked at her, Maya said, "Is your shoulder, ok? I can walk." Caden said, "I'm fine." Caden kissed her. Maya was quiet. Caden said, "I love you." Maya said, "I love you too." Caden said, "You're going to be ok." Maya was quiet. Caden kissed her. They were still walking. Emily groaned. Pacey said, "Emily, are you ok?" Emily said, "It's my ankle." Pacey said, "Let's take a short break." Caden said, "You guys can have a break, but I'm going to take her." Maya interrupted, Maya said, "You need to take a break too." Caden said, "But you really need to get to the hospital." Maya said, "Just for a minute" Caden looked at Maya, Maya said, "I'm ok, put me down." Caden put Maya on the ground, Caden groaned. Maya said, "Caden?" Caden said, "I'm ok." Maya said, "Your shoulder is hurting, you shouldn't be carrying me all day, I can walk." Caden said, "Maya, you are too weak, I know you can't walk." Maya said, "I can." Caden didn't say anything. Caden looked at Pacey. Emily was sitting with Maya, Taylor and Quinn kept looking at Maya. Maya knew they kept watching her. Maya said, "Taylor, Quinn, I am going to be ok." Quinn said, "I know." They went over to her, so they could talk to her. Caden walked over to Pacey, Caden whispered, "Maya's pale." Pacey whispered, "I know, but she's going to be ok." Caden was looking around. Caden said, "We better go now." Maya said, "Let's get some rest." Pacey said, "Let's take 5 minutes, then we can leave." Caden sighed. Maya said, "Caden, stop worrying." Caden looked at her, Caden said, "I am worried, you've lost a lot of blood." Maya said, "I will be ok." Caden was quiet. Maya said, "Pacey, can you check his shoulder?" Caden said, "Don't worry, I'm fine." Pacey said, "Caden, let me check you." Caden looked at Maya, Maya looked back at him. Pacey was checking his shoulder, Pacey said, "I think it's sprained, but you will be ok." Caden said, "I know." Emily said, "Let's go." Pacey said, "Ok." Pacey went to Emily, and helped her up, Taylor helped Quinn up too, Caden was ready to grab Maya, but Maya said, "I can walk." Caden said, "Let me carry you." Maya said, "You can't, your shoulder." Caden said, "My shoulder will be fine, you can't walk." Maya interrupted. Maya said, "I can." Pacey said, "Maya, let him." Quinn said, "You can't walk," Maya sighed. Caden got her up, they were walking. Caden was carrying her again, until they found the park. Quinn turned to Caden and Maya. Maya was asleep. Quinn said, "Maya?" Maya didn't wake up. Quinn went to Maya, Caden put Maya on the ground, they tried to wake her up. Caden said, "Pacey!" Pacey looked at them. Pacey said, "Taylor, get someone to call an ambulance." Taylor ran away. Pacey went to Maya, Pacey cried to get her to wake up, But Maya didn't wake up. Caden said, "Why isn't she waking up?" Pacey said, "She is ok, she's just very tired."

Pacey finally got Maya to wake up. Caden said, "Maya, are you ok?" Maya said, "Yeah I'm tired." Caden was crying. Caden kissed her. Taylor and some woman came over, the woman was looking at Maya, and talking to someone on the phone. Taylor said, "She's calling the police and Ambulance" Pacey said, "Thanks, Ma'am," Maya whispered, "I am so cold." Caden pulled her to him and held her, to keep her warm. Emily sat on the ground, Emily said, "Maya, an ambulance is coming, you are going to be ok." Maya whispered, "We are going to be ok." Emily said, "You are right, and the police will get A.J." Maya said, "A.J. shouldn't have done this to us." Caden said, "Frank lied to him, that's why." Maya said, "Why? We've done nothing to him." Caden said, "I know, don't worry about them." Caden kissed her, the woman said, "Is she okay?" Pacey said, "She's ok, but she really needs to go to the hospital." The lady said, "They're on the way." Pacey said, "Thanks." She said, "What happened?" Taylor explained everything to her. She said, "Why?" Pacey said, "We don't know." Quinn was looking around; Quinn was thinking about Blake. Taylor looked at her, Taylor knew that Quinn was thinking about Blake. Taylor went over to Quinn, Taylor said, "Blake's going to be ok, Blake will come back soon. Quinn said, "I'm scared." Quinn was crying. Taylor hugged her, Taylor said, "Blake can beat A.J., Blake's very strong." Quinn whispered, "Yeah." Taylor said, "The police will go out there, and get A.J." Quinn looked at her, and Quinn said, "How long will they be?" The lady said, "Just a few minutes." Quinn sighed. Taylor was whispering to Quinn. Maya groaned. Caden said, "Maya?" Maya said, "I'm ok." Caden said, "I don't think you are." Maya said, "My stomach was hurting but I'm ok," Caden kept looking at her. Caden said, "Everything will be ok." Maya said, "What about Frank?" Caden said, "Let the police take of that; Frank won't touch us." Pacey said, "Don't worry about Frank or A.J." Caden said, "They can't touch you again, because the police will get them." Pacey said, "Caden's right." Maya said, "I am worried about them hurting Caden." Caden said, "Don't, I will be fine, they won't hurt me." Pacey said, "Caden's right, because the police will get them." Maya was quiet. Maya was shivering. Caden looked at

Maya, Caden knew that she was cold. Caden held her again. Caden was trying to keep her warm. Caden said, "You are cold." Maya was quiet, Maya looked at him. Caden said, "Love you." Maya whispered, "I love you too." Caden knew Maya was very weak, because of her voice. Caden kissed her, Caden was looking around. Caden wanted the ambulance to hurry up. Caden said, "Where is the ambulance?" The woman said, "They are on their way." Pacey said, "They will be here soon, Caden." Maya whispered, "Caden." Caden looked at her. Maya whispered, "I'm ok." Caden said, "I know you are ok, I want you to go to the hospital now." Maya whisper, "I know, hold me." Caden held her tight. Caden said, "When you get better, we have to talk to Peyton." Maya said, "What about?" Caden said, "We will talk about that later." Caden still held her tight. Maya was quiet. Quinn was looking at Maya, Quinn whispered, "Maya's too weak now." Taylor said, "I know, she's lost a lot of blood." Caden was looking around again.

A.J. was lying on the ground. A.J. was panting. Blake was looking at him. Blake said, "Why do you want to hurt us? We've done nothing to you." A.J. said, "When that happened to me, you guys ignored me, you guys didn't try to help me, Frank made Caden get his phone, Caden was walking, he didn't run, Maya was worried about him, not about me, Maya kept complaining that Frank made him leave." Blake said, "Frank lied to you." A.J. said, "Don't say that." Blake interrupted. Blake said, "A.J., Frank was just trying to get you to not be friends with us, I don't know why." A.J. said, "Then why did you guys not visit me when I was in the hospital?" Blake said, "Because Frank wouldn't let us visit you, Frank blamed us, we tried to talk to Frank, but Frank hit Caden, and tried to fight me at the hospital, we tried to help you, and we wanted to see you at the hospital, but Frank wouldn't let us." A.J. sat up, AJ. said, "Frank told me that you guys didn't want to visit me, when I got there, he said the police made you guys go to the hospital, because they wanted to talk to you guys, and when They are finished with you guys. Parker and Trey were laughing. They thought it was funny that those men beat me, and I couldn't beat them," Blake said, "No, they never said that." A.J. said, "Then you guys walked away, and didn't even try to see me, or anything" Blake said, "We tried! Frank wouldn't let us when you got out of the hospital. Remember, Quinn and I was trying to hide it from Frank, that we went to see you?" A.J. said, "I remember." Blake said, "Because Frank wouldn't let us, we wanted to see you, we decided to sneak, and see you." A.J. kept looking at Blake. A.J. said, "Why would Frank do that?" Blake said, "I don't know, you need to ask Frank about that." A.J. said, "And I was in love Maya." Blake was shocked. Blake looked at A.J. Blake said, "Then why did you try to get Caden to ask her out?" AJ. said, "I didn't want you guys to know, I planned to ask her out when we got back, I knew that Caden wouldn't have asked her out that day until Frank told me that Maya didn't care about me, and that she cared about Caden more. I stopped loving her, I wanted to hurt her!" Blake said, "We didn't know that you were in love to Maya, but Maya did care about you. Maya loved you as a brother." A.J. said, "I don't think so." Blake said, "You don't need to let." A.J. interrupted and said, "I thought you all my best friends, but I was wrong." Blake said, "We were your best friends." A.J. said "But you guys didn't act like it." Blake said, "We tried, but Frank wouldn't let us, I told you this many times." A.J. kept looking at him. Blake said, "We did care about you, Maya loved you as brother, Frank wouldn't let us go around you, Frank blamed me and Caden because we let you go in the woods alone, you told Caden that you didn't need him to go with him." A.J. said, "If I told him no, he should've ignored me, and came with me anyway." Blake said, "You sound like Frank." A.J. said, "I wanted you guys to pay back." Blake said, "Frank told you to hurt us." A.J. said, "No, Frank doesn't know I am here," Blake said, "Then why did Frank come out here, and try to go with us?" AJ. said, "He wanted to hurt you all too. He wanted to come out, so he could hurt you all." Blake said, "Why did you let Frank get to you? Frank lied to you a lot." A.J. said, "No, you lied, Frank wouldn't lie to me." Blake sighed. Blake said, "I'm not going to stay and talk to you about Frank, Frank lied to you, I better get out of here." Blake got up. A.J. said, "You think I'm going to let you go?" Blake said, "You can't make me stay with you, I'm going to my friends, they need me." Blake started walking away. A.J. grabbed a tree stick, then ran to Blake, hit his back with it, Blake went to the ground. A.J. kept hitting Blake's back, A.J. said, "I told you I wouldn't let you go! I'm going to get your little friends too!" Blake grabbed the stick and pulled it away from him. A.J. went to him, they started fighting again. Blake beat him, A.J. went to the ground. A.J. was panting. Blake got up; Blake groaned. Blake said, "Leave me alone." A.J. said, "Never!" A.J. grabbed the knife from his pocket, Blake didn't notice that. A.J. went to him. They went to the ground again and fought. A.J. slashed Blake's stomach with the knife, Blake went to the ground, and groaned. A.J. got up. A.J. looked at Blake. And said, "I told you that you couldn't beat me." A.J. was ready stab him again, but Blake kicked him, A.J. went to the ground again, and dropped the knife. Blake went over to A.J. They fought again, A.J. finally got away from Blake, AJ. got up, and was looking at Blake, Blake was panting, Blake saw the knife, Blake reached on the ground to get the knife. A.J. saw him, A.J. ran toward him, AJ. tripped, and fell on top of Blake, and groaned, Blake could see that A.J. had been stabbed in the side, Blake pushed A.J. away from him, Blake was looking at A.J., AJ. was looking at his side. Blake got up. Blake kicked A.J.'s face. A.J. passed out. Blake sat down and looked at him. Blake was waiting for the police to come. Blake knew that Pacey and Caden got the police to come. Blake was looking around, he waited for the police for a while. Finally, the police came. Blake looked at them. The policeman said, "Blake Lawton?" Blake said, "I'm Blake, that's A.J." Blake pointed at A.J. the other policeman went to A.J. He checked A.J., the officer said, "He's going to be ok; He needs to see the doctor." The other officer said, "Do you know why he would want to do this to you?" Blake said, "He thought we didn't care about him, he wanted us to get pay back." The officer looked at him. And said, "You need to see the doctor too, after that, we will talk about all this." Blake was looking at A.J. The officers woke A.J. up. A.J. groaned. A.J. looked at the police then at Blake. A.J. said, "You got them here." Blake said, "I told you Caden, and Pacey told them where we were?' They got A.J. up. A.J. said, "I will be back." Blake was looking at A.J.

Quinn was walking around in the lobby. Pacey, Taylor, Emily, and Caden were sitting down. Emily's ankle was sprained, she has to use crutches, and Caden's shoulder is sprained, so he has to wear a sling on his arm. They were waiting for the doctor to come and let them know about Maya. Caden was nervous. Pacey said, "Caden, Maya's fine." Caden said, "She's very weak." Pacey said, "I know, she's lost a lot of blood, that's why." Caden said, "You think Maya will be, ok?" Pacey said, "I told you many times Maya's going to be ok." Caden was looking around. Pacey said, "Quinn, I know Blake's okay." Quinn said, "Why is Blake not here yet?" Pacey said, "Maybe the police wanted to talk to him." Caden said, "Maybe Blake's on his way." Quinn sighed. Quinn sat down. Quinn said, "I want to see Blake right now." Caden said, "I wanted to see Maya too, right now, but they wouldn't let me." Pacey said, "Have you talk to her mother?" Caden said, "They are on their way." Pacey said,

"Good." Caden said, "Mrs. Post is going to freak out." Pacey said, "I know she will." Caden was looking around, Pacey said, "And I know you feel bad, because you couldn't protect her, but it's not your fault." Caden looked at him. Pacey said, "It's not your fault, you were trying to get A.J. to stop, and by doing that you were protecting her." Caden was quiet. A nurse came in the lobby, the nurse said, "Pacey Wheeler?" Pacey looked at the nurse. Pacey said, "That's me." Nurse said, "Someone, wants to talk to you." Pacey said, "Who?" Nurse said, "I don't know his name, I will show you where he his." Pacey said, "Guys, I'll be right back." Pacey kissed Taylor, then started following the nurse. They went to the emergency room, the nurse pointed at a room, Pacey went to that room, Pacey saw Blake. Pacey said, "Blake?" Blake said, "Pacey, is Quinn, ok?" Pacey said, "She's fine, she is worried about you, why didn't you let her know you're here?" Blake said, "I don't want her to see me like this, when they are done with me, I'll go tell her." Pacey looked at his face, and stomach. Pacey said, "Are you ok?" Blake said, "I will be ok" Pacey said, "Where's A.J.?" Blake said, "I think in the other room." Pacey said, "What happened?" Blake explained what had happened to him. Pacey said "Why did Frank lie to A.J.?" Blake said, "I don't know. I told the police about Frank, I had to, I don't want Frank to try to hurt Quinn," Pacey said, "I know, Quinn's really worried about you, I think she needs to know right now." Blake said, "Give me 15 minutes, I will be there." Pacey sighed. Blake said, "You know how she is, if she knows, she will panic. I don't want her to see me like this." Pacey said, "You're right." Blake said, "Are you sure Quinn is ok?" Pacey said, "She's okay." Blake said, "Maya?" Pacey said, "Maya's with the doctor, we are waiting for the doctor." Blake said, "Do you think Maya's ok?" Pacey said, "I think so, I didn't know that A.J. was in love with her." Blake said, "Me either." They talked for a while, then the nurse came in. Pacey said, "I better go wait in the lobby, and check on Taylor." Blake said, "I will be there in few minutes." Pacey said, "What do you want me to say when Quinn asks me who wanted to see me?" Blake said, "Let her know I'm here, and I'm ok." Pacey said, "See you in a few minutes." Pacey walked back to his friends and sat down. Pacey looked around the lobby for Caden. Pacey said, "Where's Caden?" Taylor said, "With Maya, Maya's going to be in the hospital for a few days, but she's going to be ok." Pacey said, "I knew she was going to be ok." Taylor said, "Me too, who wanted to see you?" Pacey said, "Blake." Quinn said, "Blake? Blake is here. Why didn't he want to see me?" Pacey said, "He's ok. He has to see the doctor first." Quinn said, "Is he hurt?" Pacey said, "He's ok." Quinn said, "But why doesn't he want to see me?" Pacey said, "I don't know. Ask him later." Quinn said, "Are you sure that he's, ok?" Pacey said, "He's fine, he was worried about you, that's why he wanted to see me, he wanted to ask me if you were ok." Quinn said, "He should've asked them to get me," Pacey said, "Quinn, I know he should've, but he knew if you went in there and saw him, you would freak out." Quinn said, "Is he hurt bad?" Pacey said, "No." Quinn was getting ready to say something, but Blake interrupted. Blake said, "Quinn." Quinn looked at him, Quinn got up and went to him, Quinn said, "Blake?" Blake said, "Are you ok?" Quinn said, "I'm fine, you are not ok." Blake said, "I will be ok, I need to sit down, my back's hurting." Blake went to the chair and sat down. Blake groaned. Quinn sat with him. Blake said, "We are okay." Emily said, "Where is A.J.?" Blake said, "In the emergency room." Taylor said, "What happened?" Blake explained everything to them, everything. Caden said, "A.J.'s in love with Maya?" Everyone looked at him. Taylor said, "How is Maya?" Caden said, "She hasn't woken up, but they said that she's going to be ok." Taylor said, "I'm glad she's ok." Caden said, "Me too, I'm not going to let A.J. touch her ever again." Blake said, "A.J. won't." Caden said, "I didn't know that

A.J. was in love with her, but why did he try to get me to talk to her?" Blake said, "A.J. didn't want us to know, that he planned to ask her out when we got back, but then A.J. got jumped, and Frank lied to him about us," Caden said, "I am going to get Frank!" Blake said, "You don't need to." Caden said, "Frank got Maya hurt." Blake said, "I know, but Maya's going to be ok." Caden was angry. Blake said, "And the police are going to talk to him." Caden said, "I'm going to stay with Maya all night." Pacey said, "We will be at the motel, if you need anything, let us know." Caden said, "I will." Quinn said, "We will come see Maya tomorrow." Caden said, "I will let Maya know." Emily grabbed her crutches, then got up. Blake said, "Emily, is your ankle, okay?" Emily said, "My ankle's okay, but it's sprained," Blake was looking at Caden's shoulder. Blake said, "Your shoulder?" Caden said, "It's sprained too, are you okay?" Blake said. "I will be ok." Caden said, "I better go to Maya. See you guys tomorrow." Caden walked to Maya's room. Caden saw that Maya had woken up. Caden said, "Maya." Caden went over to Maya. Maya said, "Caden, are you ok?" Caden said, "I'm fine, how do you feel?" Maya said, "I'm so tired." Caden said, "I know." Caden kissed her, Caden said, "Go to sleep." Maya said, "Where is A.J.?" Caden said, "A.J. is in the emergency room now." Maya said, "Blake's, ok?" Caden said, "Everyone is ok, they are going to a motel, they will see you tomorrow," Maya said, "Why is A.J. in the emergency room?" Caden explained everything to her. Maya was shocked. Maya said, "A.J. was in love with me?" Caden said, "Yeah AJ. told Blake." Maya said, "I didn't know." Caden said, "I'm glad that you didn't date him." Maya said, "He's not my type, you are my type." Caden kissed her. Caden said, "Go to sleep, you need to get more rest."

Caden was sitting on the hospital bed, talking to Maya. Maya said, "I hate hospitals," Caden said, "Everyone hates hospitals." Maya pulled Caden to her. They hugged, Maya said, "Thank you." Caden said, "What for?" Maya said, "You was there for me." Caden said, "I will always be there for you." Maya smiled. Caden kissed her. Maya said, "We have to do something about Erin." Caden said, "I will talk ta Peyton about that." Maya said, "No, I don't want Peyton to be involved in this" Caden said, "She is now. Erin and Peyton almost fought, and Erin was afraid of Peyton." Quinn interrupted them, Quinn said, "Maya." Maya and Caden looked at Quinn, Emily, and Taylor. Caden got up, to let them talk to Maya. Caden said, "We will talk about that later, Maya." Maya said, "But I still don't want Peyton to do that." Quinn said, "You don't need to worry about Erin, you need to get rest." Caden said, "Maya, Quinn's right." Maya looked at him. Caden said, "I won't let her get to us again." Caden kissed her. Quinn said, "Maya, you feel ok?" Maya said, "I'm ok now." Caden said, "But you still feel tired, and weak," Maya said, "A little, but I feel ok." Emily sat on the chair. Caden said, "Where is Blake and Pacey?" Quinn said, "In the waiting area. They needed to talk." Caden said, "I'm going out there to talk to them, Maya if you need me, get Quinn or Taylor to come get me." Maya said, "I will." Caden kissed Maya, then walked Blake and Pacey. Caden said, "Everything ok?" Blake said, "Frank was here, we made the girls go to Maya, we wanted to make sure that Frank wouldn't go around you guys, and the girls." Caden said, "Where's Frank?" Blake said, "He went to A.J. now." Caden said, "Frank better not try to do anything to Maya." Blake said, "I don't think Frank will try to do anything to us now." Caden said, "If Frank is trying." Pacey interrupted. Pacey said, "Frank, what do you want?" Caden turned to Frank. Frank said, "If I am trying what?" Caden said, "If you are trying to hurt Maya again, I'm going to come after you." Frank said, "You guys hurt A.J., I'm going to get you all to pay back." Caden looked at Frank. Blake said, "We did not try to hurt him, he came after us." Frank looked at Caden, Frank said, "I will get Maya very soon." Blake said, "Leave Maya alone." Frank said, "I won't, then it will be you all." Caden grabbed Frank, Caden said, "If you touch her, I am coming after you and." Blake interrupted. Blake said, "Caden, don't." Caden interrupted. Caden said, "Blake, let me go." Frank kept talking to Caden, Frank made Caden angry, Caden hit Frank, Frank went to the floor, Frank touched his jaw. And laughed. Caden was ready to go to Frank again, but Blake and Pacey pulled Caden away from him, they went to Maya's room. Caden was angry. Blake said, "Calm down." Caden looked at him, then at Maya. Maya knew something was wrong. Maya said, "What's wrong?" Caden said, "Nothing." Maya said, "Why are you mad?" Caden said, "I'm not mad." Maya said, "I'm not stupid, why?" Caden was quiet. Maya said, "Caden?" Pacey said, "We were talking to Frank, Frank made him mad." Maya said, "Caden, are you ok? Did he hurt you?" Blake said, "He's fine. He hit Frank." Maya said, "What did Frank do that made Caden angry?" Blake and Pacey looked at each other. Caden said, "Frank's going to try to come after you." Maya looked at Caden. Caden said, "I don't know what I would do if Frank hurt you." Maya said, "Caden, I'm going to be fine. The police will not let him come around me." Caden said, "If he gets to you, I will hurt him" Maya said, "Forget him, I will be fine, Frank won't come around me." Caden was quiet. Maya said, "We will talk to the police." Caden kept looking at Maya. Pacey said, "I think Frank wants to make you angry. I don't think Frank will actually try to hurt Maya." Caden said, "Frank better not come around Maya." Maya said, "We are going to be fine." Caden said, "You are right." Caden went to Maya. Caden said, "Love you." Maya said, "Love you too." Caden kissed her.

Everyone was looking at Caden, and Maya. They were worried about Caden and Maya.

Frank overheard them. Frank was laughing, Frank said, "I will see you all very soon." Frank walked away. Quinn said, "Let's not talk about Frank or A.J. we don't want to talk about them again." Maya said, "You're right, Quinn." Caden said, "We won't talk about them, Maya, are you hungry?" Maya said, "I'm starving." Caden said, "What kind of food do you want to eat?" Maya said, "Anything, what about you?" Caden said, "I'm thinking about Taco bell. I know your favorite is Taco Bell." Maya said, "You know what I always eat there." Caden smiled, Caden said, "I will get it, what kind of drink?" Maya said, "Water." Caden said, "Ok, I will be back." Caden kissed her. Caden said, "Love you." Maya said, "Love you too." Blake said, "Caden, I'm going with you." Caden looked at Blake, Caden knew that Blake thought he was going to try to go after Frank. Caden said, "Pacey, can you stay here and watch Maya until I get back?" Pacey said, "I can stay." Maya said, "No, I'm fine." Caden looked at Maya, then at Pacey. Pacey said, "I will stay here." Caden said, "Thanks," Pacey knew that Caden was afraid that Frank would come back and try to hurt her. Caden and Blake walked away. Maya said, "I know Caden wanted you to stay, because of Frank, right?" Pacey said, "I think so." Maya said, "Frank won't come in here." Pacey said, "We don't know that." Maya was quiet. Quinn, Emily, and Taylor kept looking at Maya. They were scared. Maya caught them, Maya knew that they were worried. Maya said, "I'm fine." Quinn said, "I know." Taylor went over to Pacey, Taylor whispered, "Do you think Frank will come after her?" Pacey whispered, "I think he'll try." Taylor whispered, "What are we going to do?" Pacey said, "Let the police take care of that. Caden is going to talk them." Maya groaned. Taylor looked at her. Taylor said, "Are you ok?" Maya said, "I will be fine, when I tried to move, it's hurt." Taylor said, "Do you need anything?" Maya said, "No, thanks, Pacey, I wanted to know what Frank said to Caden?" Pacey explained everything to her. Maya said, "We tried to talk to the police." Pacey said, "We do need to, I'm afraid that Caden will go after Frank." Maya said, "Me too, we need to try to get Caden away from Frank." Pacey said, "But how? You know how he is; he won't let us stop him. He doesn't want to see you get hurt, he will do anything to stop him." Frank interrupted. Frank said, "Maya." They looked at Frank. Pacey went over to Frank. Pacey said, "Get out." Frank said, "I want to talk to Maya." Maya looked at Frank. Pacey said, "No, I'm never going to let you talk to her." Frank said, "Maya, I will see you very soon. You hurt A.J,, A.J. loved you." Maya was quiet. Maya kept looking at Frank. She was scared. Pacey pushed Frank away. Pacey said, "Maya did not try to hurt A.J., Maya had no idea that A.J. loved her. A.J. did try to help Caden and Maya get together. It's his fault, not Caden or Maya's, go away."

Frank still wouldn't leave. Quinn said, "I'm going to call the police." Frank looked at Quinn, then at Maya. Frank said, "I will be back, Maya." Frank walked away. Quinn called the police. Pacey turned to Maya. Taylor and Emily were looking at Maya. Pacey said, "Are you ok?" Maya said, "I'm fine." Maya looked at her friends. Maya said, "I don't want Caden to know what happened." Pacey said, "Caden has to know." Maya said, "If he knows, he goes after Frank, I don't want him to." Taylor said, "You are right." Maya said, "I don't want Caden to know about that." Pacey was quiet. They were waiting for the police for a while, Mrs. Post came into Maya's room. Mrs. Post said, "Maya, how do you feel?" Maya was getting ready to speak, but the policeman said, "Maya Post?" Everyone looked at him. Taylor said, "It's her." The policeman went over to Maya. They were talking. Mrs. Post was quiet, she heard everything. She was shocked. The policeman said, "We are going to take care of that." Maya said, "Thank you." The policeman walked away. Mrs. Post said, "I'm going to talk to Frank!" Caden and Blake came in. They heard Mrs. Post. Caden said, "Why do you want to go to him?" Everyone looked at Caden, and Blake. Mrs. Post was ready to speak, but Maya interrupted, Maya said, "Frank told you that he was going to see me soon." Caden said, "That's why the police are here?" Maya said, "I had to talk to them about that." Caden kept looking at her. Caden said, "Did he come in here after I left?" Maya said, "No, he didn't come in here, why would you think that?" Caden said, "I had to make sure." Mrs. Post looked at Maya, then at Caden. Mrs. Post knew that Maya didn't want him to know. Caden went over to Maya, Caden said, "I missed you." Maya said, "Missed you too." They kissed and Caden gave her a taco bell. Maya said, "Thanks." Maya smiled. Mrs. Post kept looking at them.

www.ingramcontent.com/pod-product-compliance
Lightning Source LLC
LaVergne TN
LVHW060142080526
838202LV00049B/4061